THE REAL POOP ON PIGEONS!

A TOON BOOK BY

KEVIN McCLOSKEY

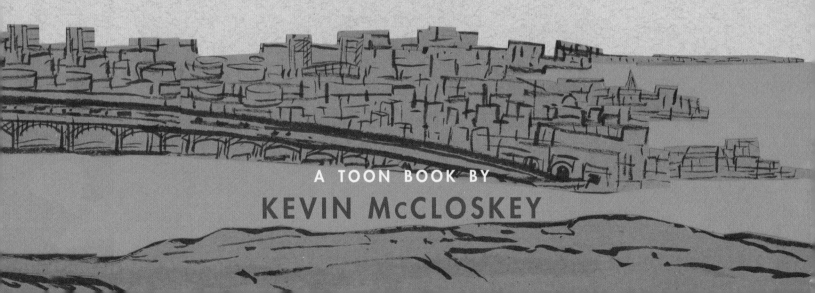

FOR ZOE AND DANIEL, OUR KIDS, WHO GREW AND FLEW.
TIME FLIES!

Editorial Director & Designer: FRANÇOISE MOULY

KEVIN McCLOSKEY'S artwork was painted with acrylics and gouache.

A JUNIOR LIBRARY GUILD SELECTION

A TOON Book™ © 2015 Kevin McCloskey & TOON Books, an imprint of RAW Junior, LLC, 27 Greene Street, New York, NY 10013. No part of this book may be used or reproduced in any manner whatsoever without written permission except in the case of brief quotations embodied in critical articles and reviews. TOON Graphics™, TOON Books®, LITTLE LIT® and TOON Into Reading!™ are trademarks of RAW Junior, LLC. All rights reserved. Historic pigeon prints are reproduced from Kevin McCloskey's personal collection: on the cover, chromolithographs by K . Wagner from a German encyclopedia, circa 1890; the Jacobins on the 'about the author page' are from Emil Schachtzabel's 1906 *Illustriertes Prachtwerk sämtlicher Taubenrassen*. All our books are Smyth Sewn (the highest library-quality binding available) and printed with soy-based inks on acid-free, woodfree paper harvested from responsible sources. Printed in China by C&C Offset Printing Co., Ltd. Distributed to the trade by Consortium Book Sales; orders (800) 283-3572; orderentry@perseusbooks.com; www.cbsd.com. Library of Congress Cataloging-in-Publication Data: McCloskey, Kevin, author, illustrator. The Real Poop on Pigeons! : A TOON Book / by Kevin McCloskey. pages cm ISBN 978-1-935179-93-1   1. Pigeons.   I. Title.   SF465.M39   2016   636.5'96--dc23   2015030551
ISBN 978-1-935179-93-1 (hardcover)
16 17 18 19 20 21 C&C 10 9 8 7 6 5 4 3 2 1
www.TOON-BOOKS.com

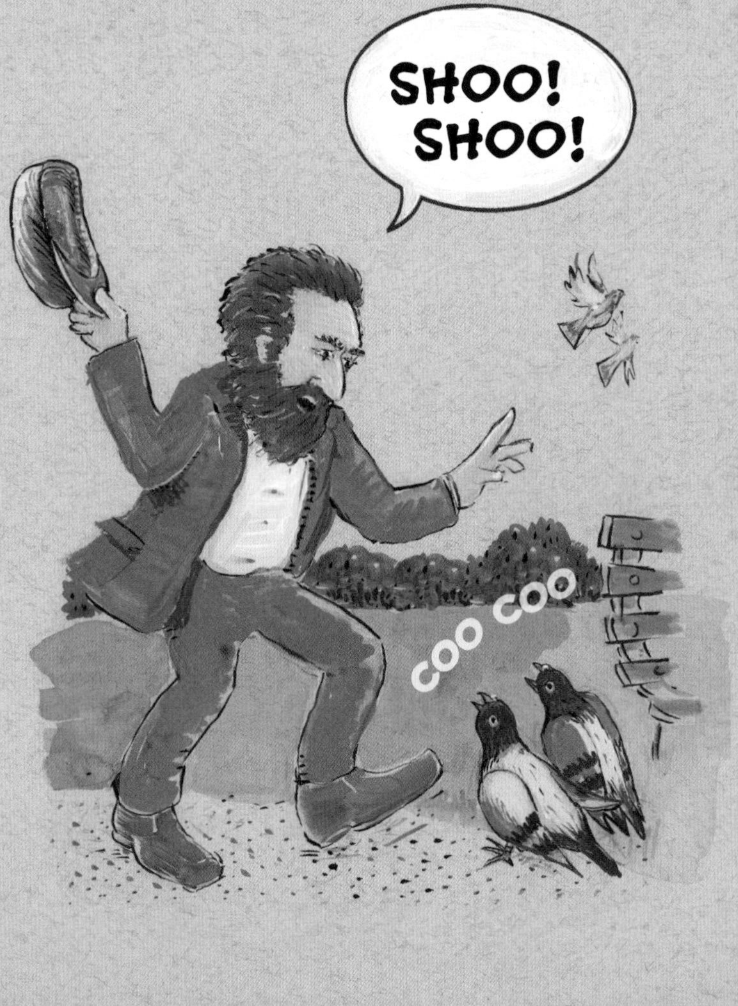
SHOO!
SHOO!
COO COO

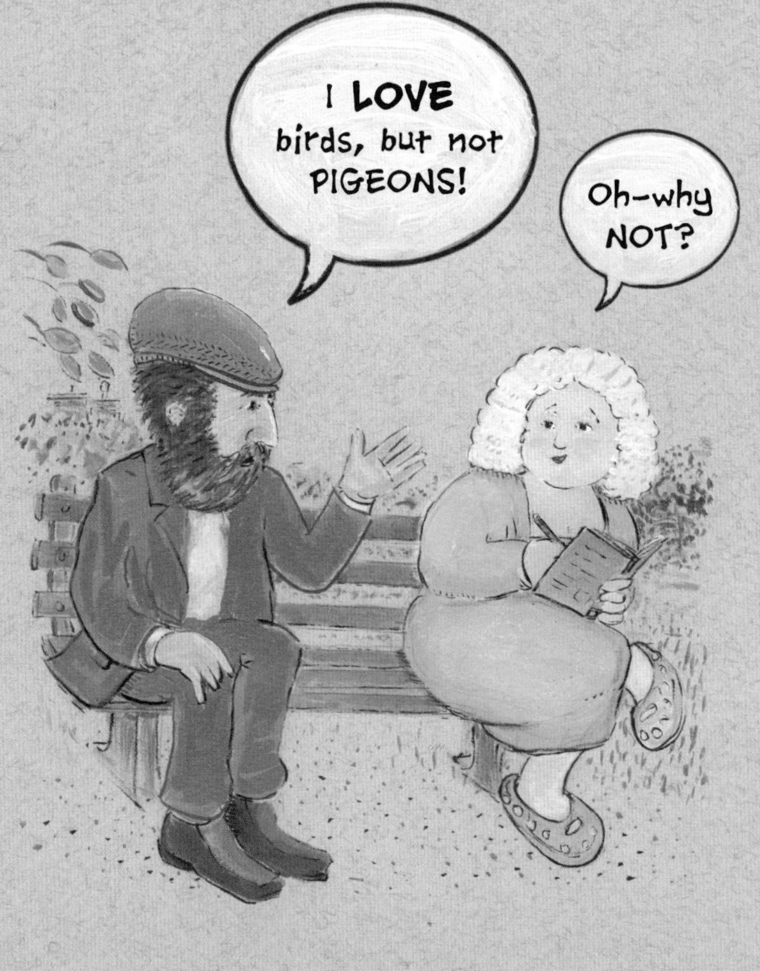
I LOVE
birds, but not
PIGEONS!
Oh-why
NOT?

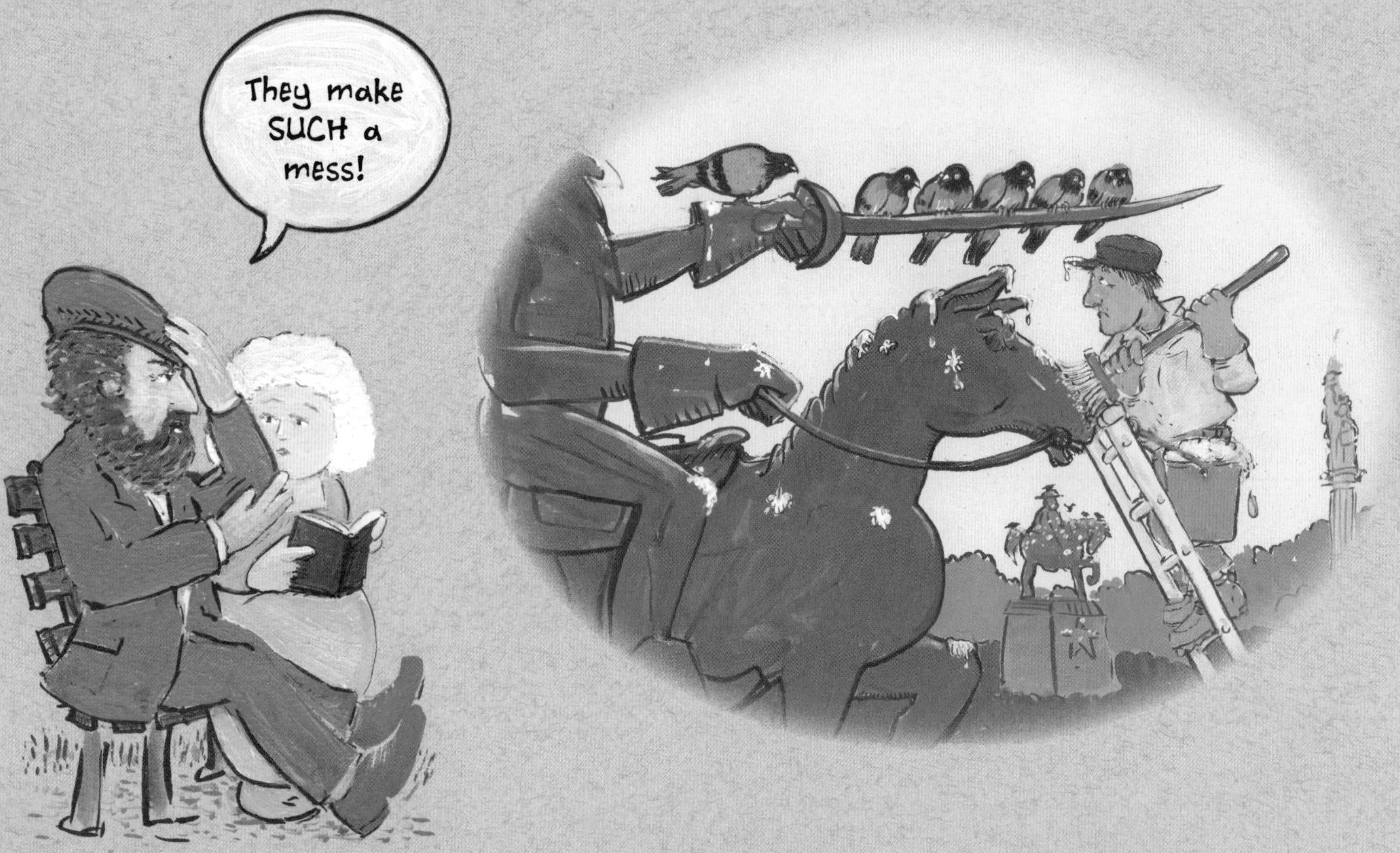
They make SUCH a mess!

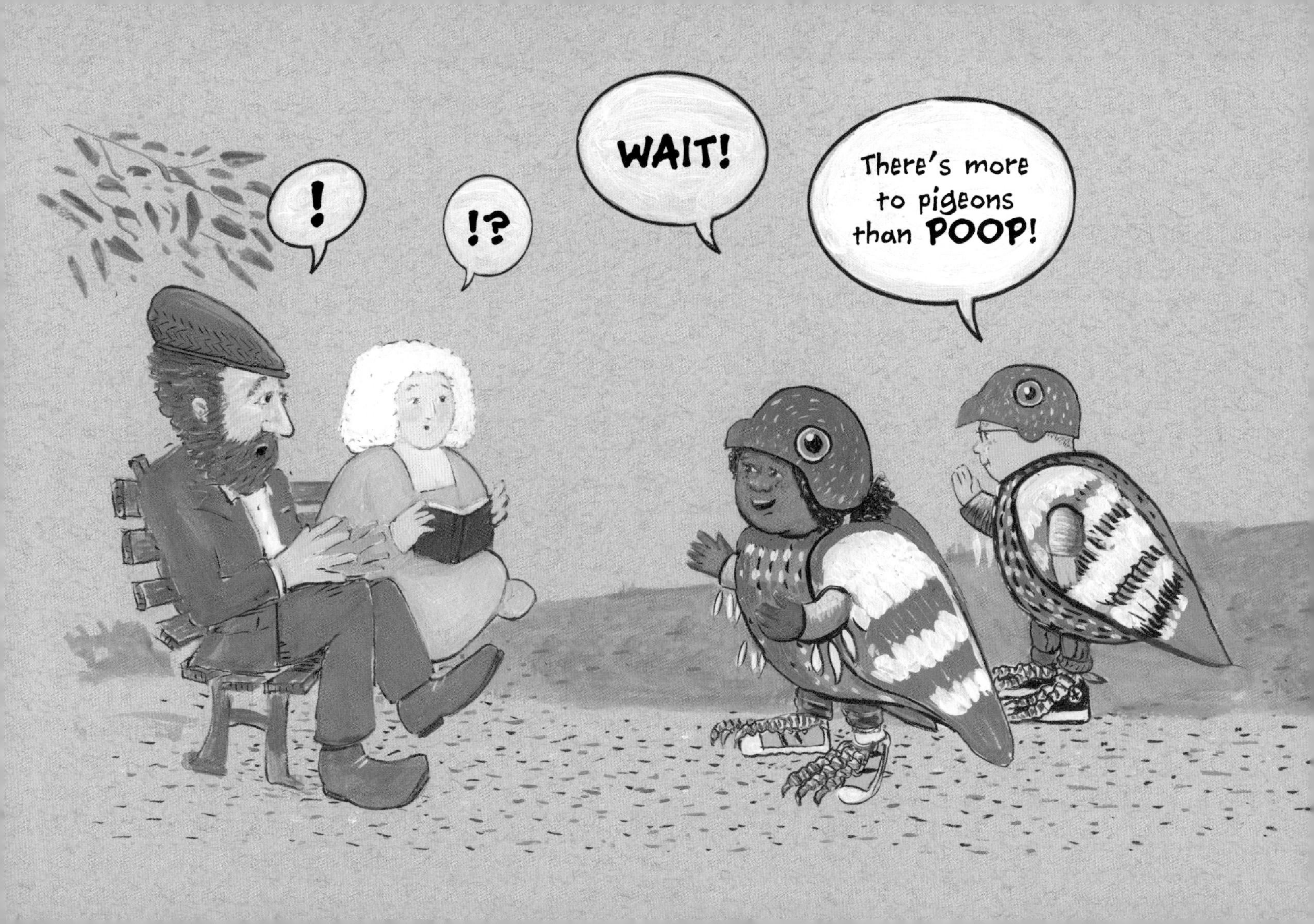
!
!?
WAIT!
There's more to pigeons than POOP!

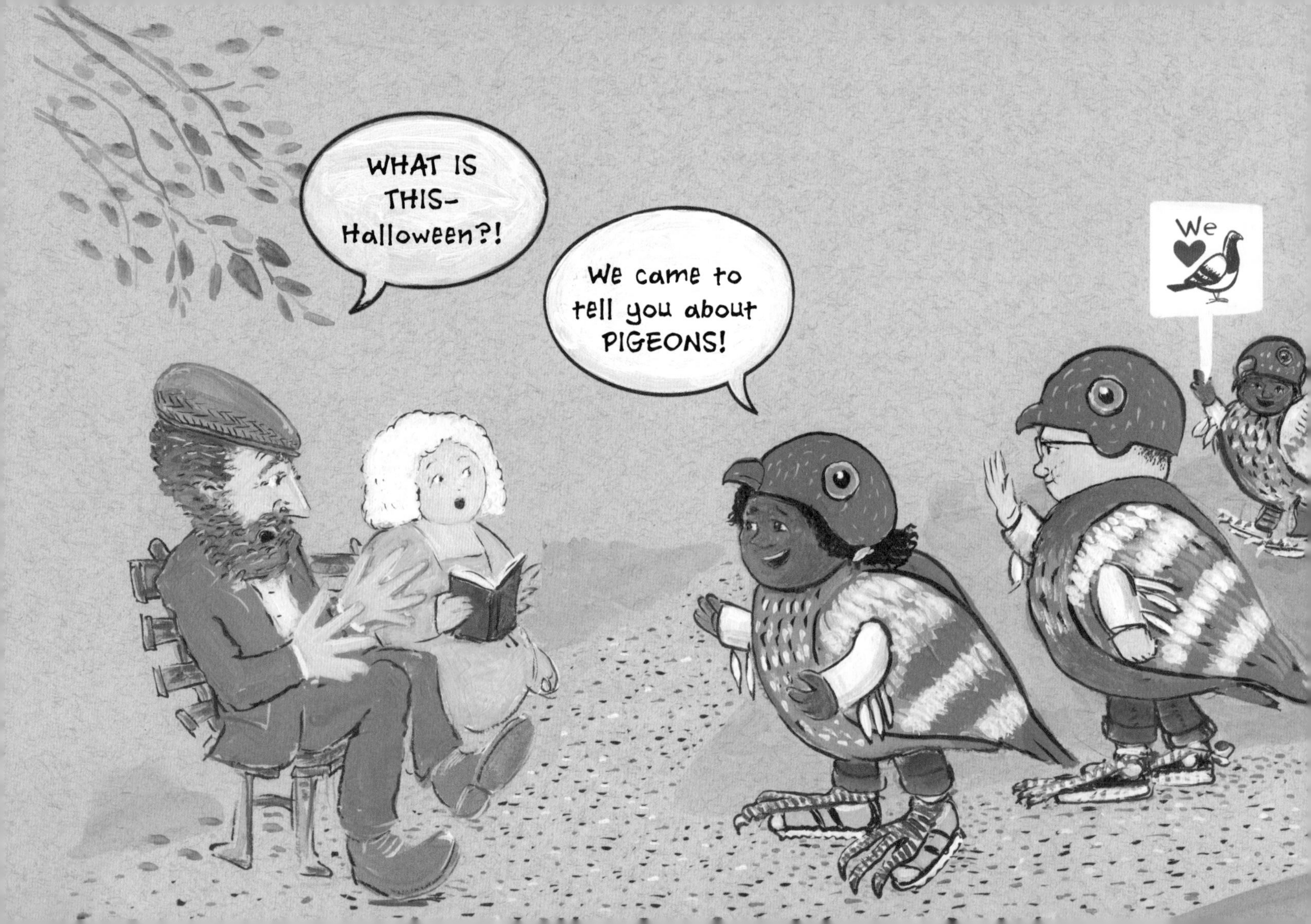
WHAT IS THIS- Halloween?!
We came to tell you about PIGEONS!
We

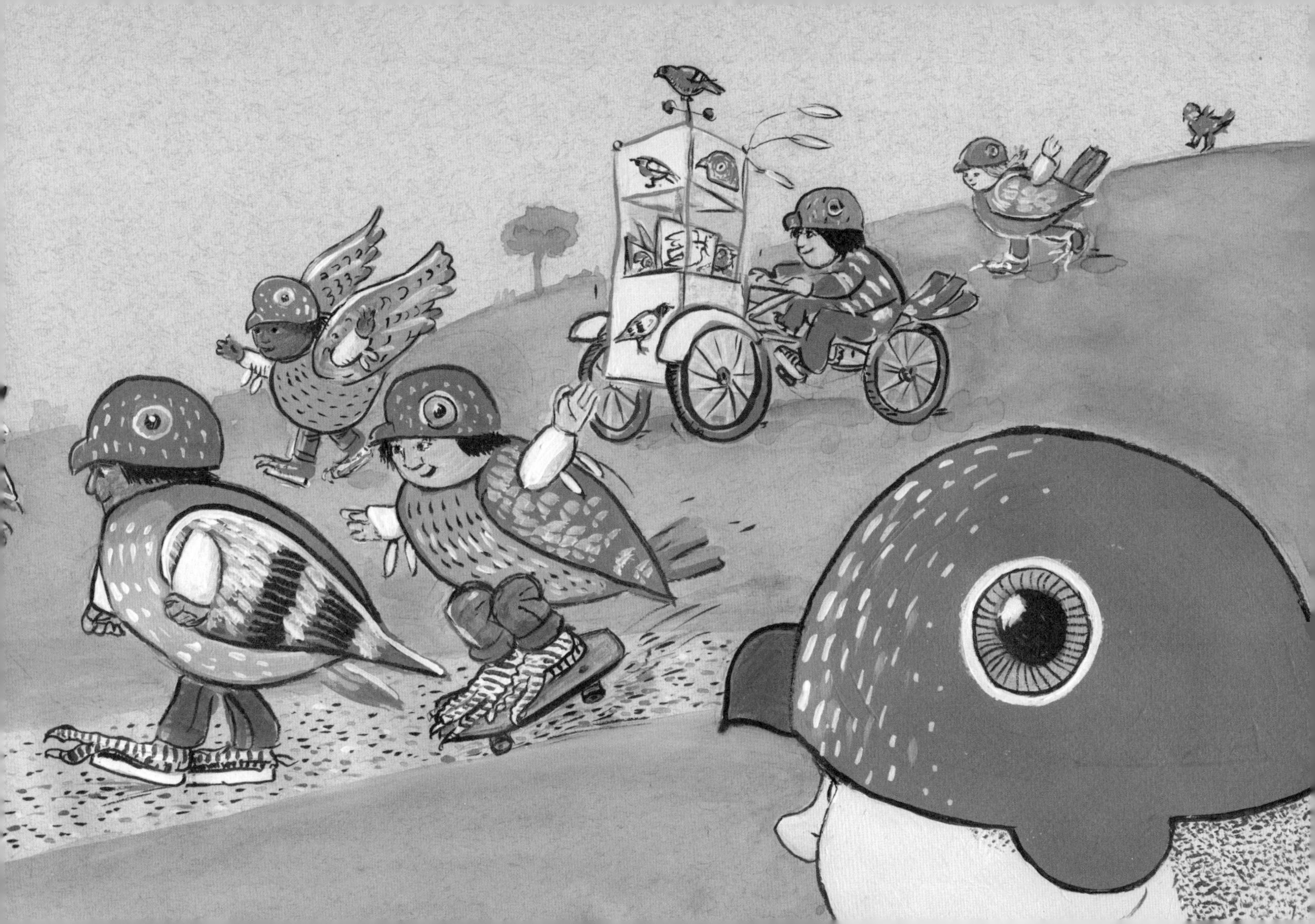

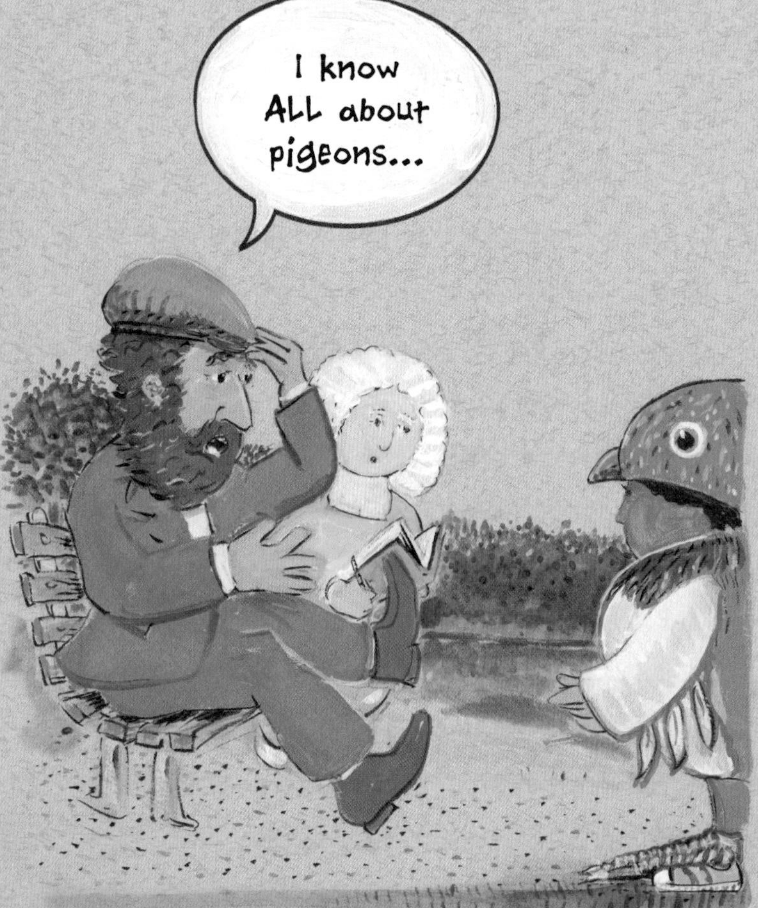
I know ALL about pigeons...

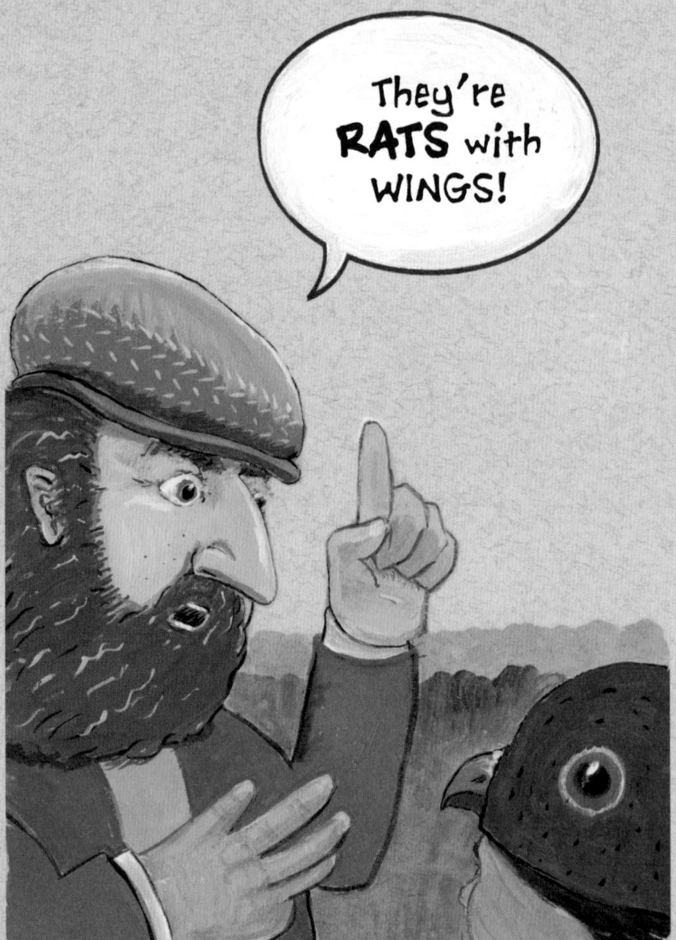
They're RATS with WINGS!

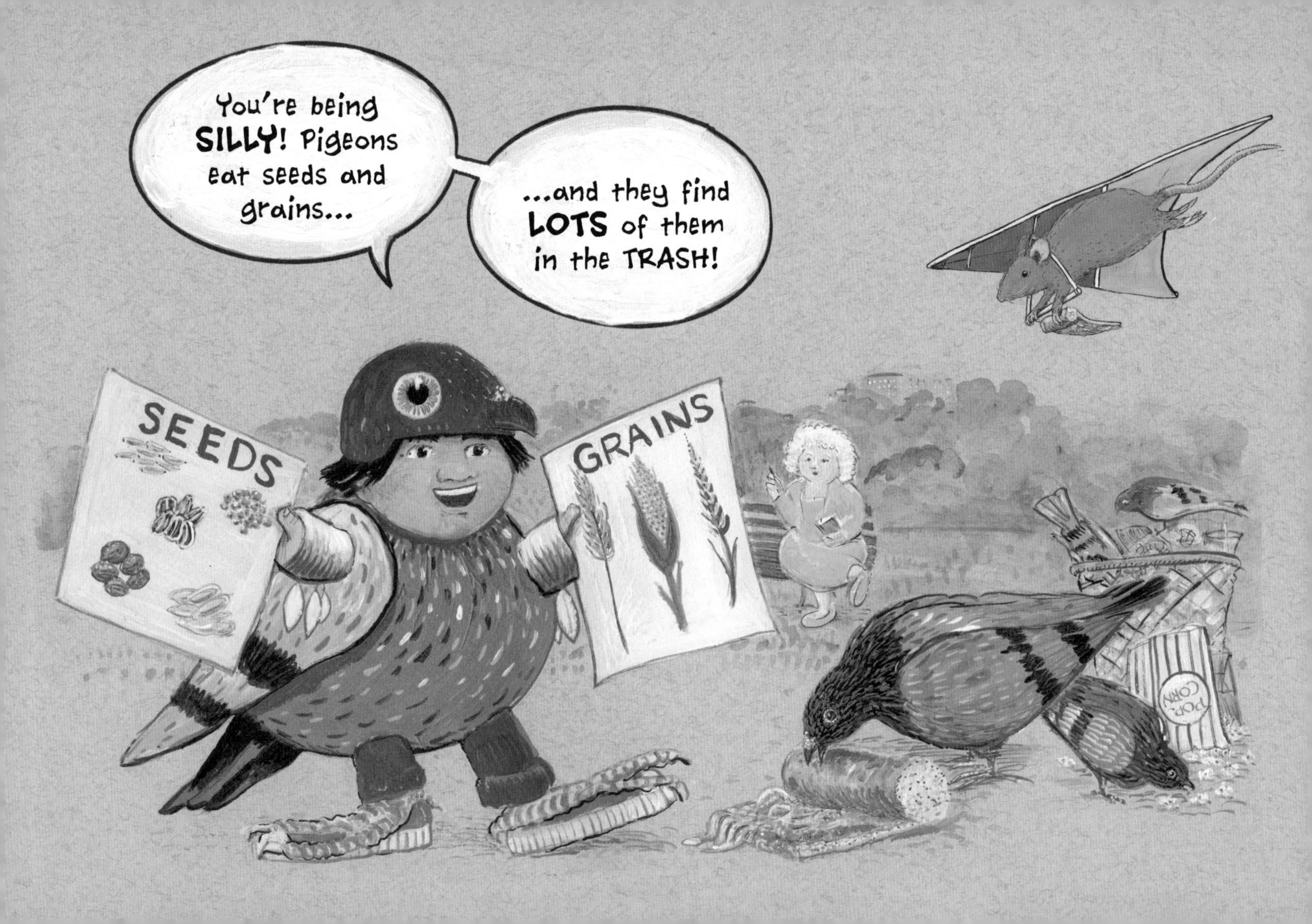
You're being SILLY! Pigeons eat seeds and grains...
...and they find LOTS of them in the TRASH!
SEEDS
GRAINS
POP CORN

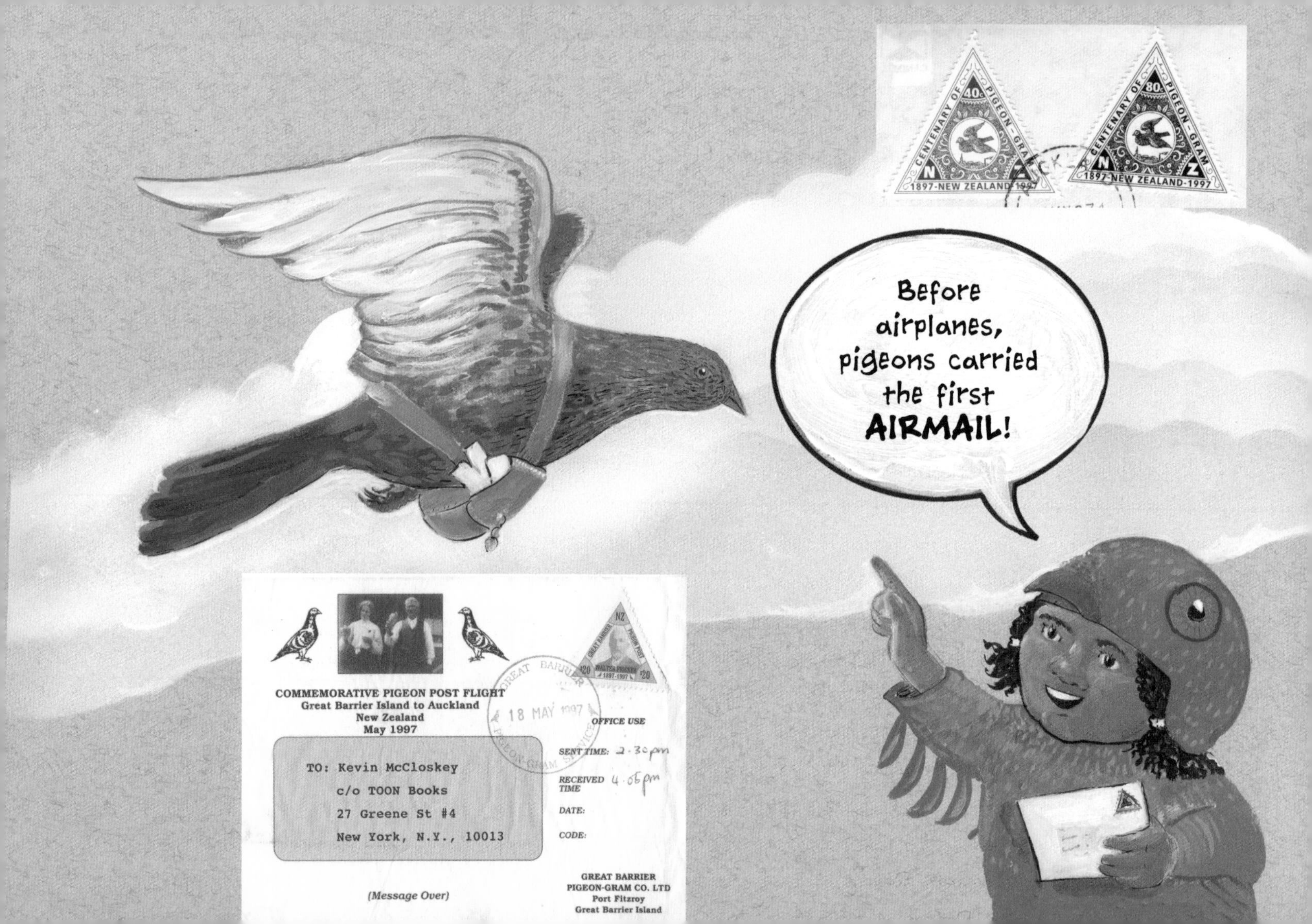
Before airplanes, pigeons carried the first **AIRMAIL!**
CENTENARY OF PIGEON-GRAM
1897-NEW ZEALAND-1997
COMMEMORATIVE PIGEON POST FLIGHT
Great Barrier Island to Auckland
New Zealand
May 1997
TO: Kevin McCloskey
c/o TOON Books
27 Greene St #4
New York, N.Y., 10013
18 MAY 1997
OFFICE USE
SENT TIME: 2.30pm
RECEIVED TIME 4.05pm
DATE:
CODE:
(Message Over)
GREAT BARRIER
PIGEON-GRAM CO. LTD
Port Fitzroy
Great Barrier Island

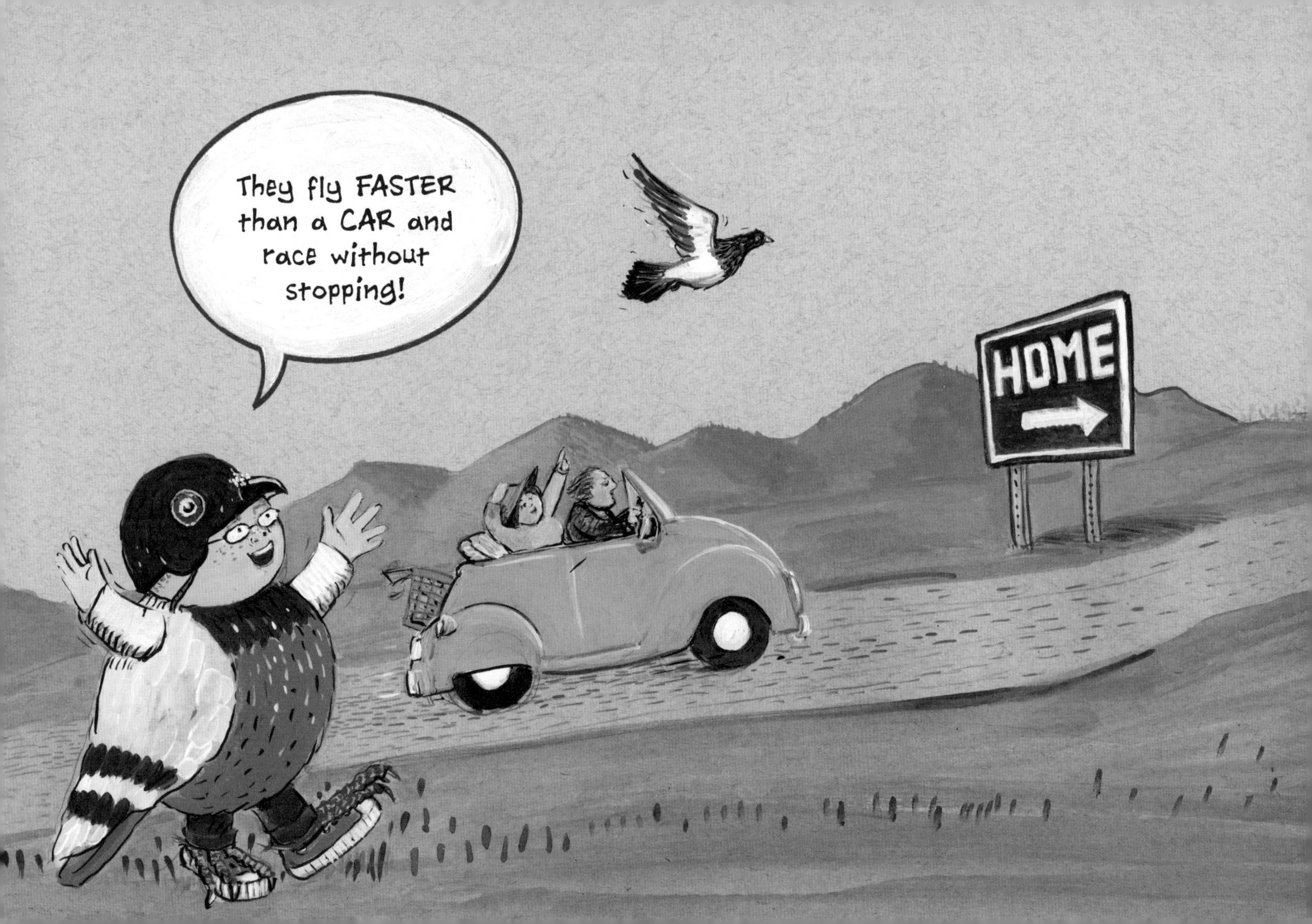
They fly FASTER than a CAR and race without stopping!
HOME

PIGEONS ARE IN THE SAME FAMILY AS DOVES.

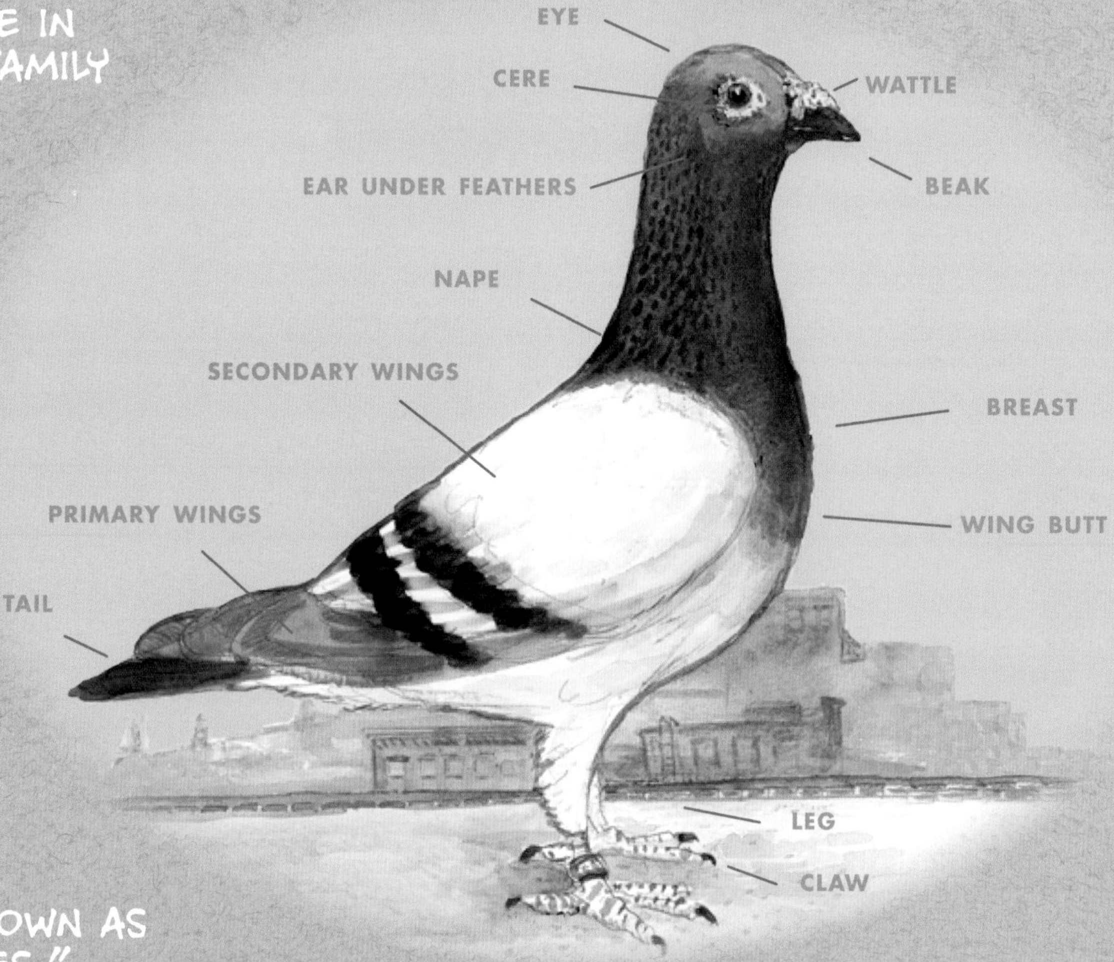
EYE
CERE
WATTLE
EAR UNDER FEATHERS
BEAK
NAPE
SECONDARY WINGS
BREAST
PRIMARY WINGS
WING BUTT
TAIL
LEG
CLAW

THEY'RE KNOWN AS "ROCK DOVES."

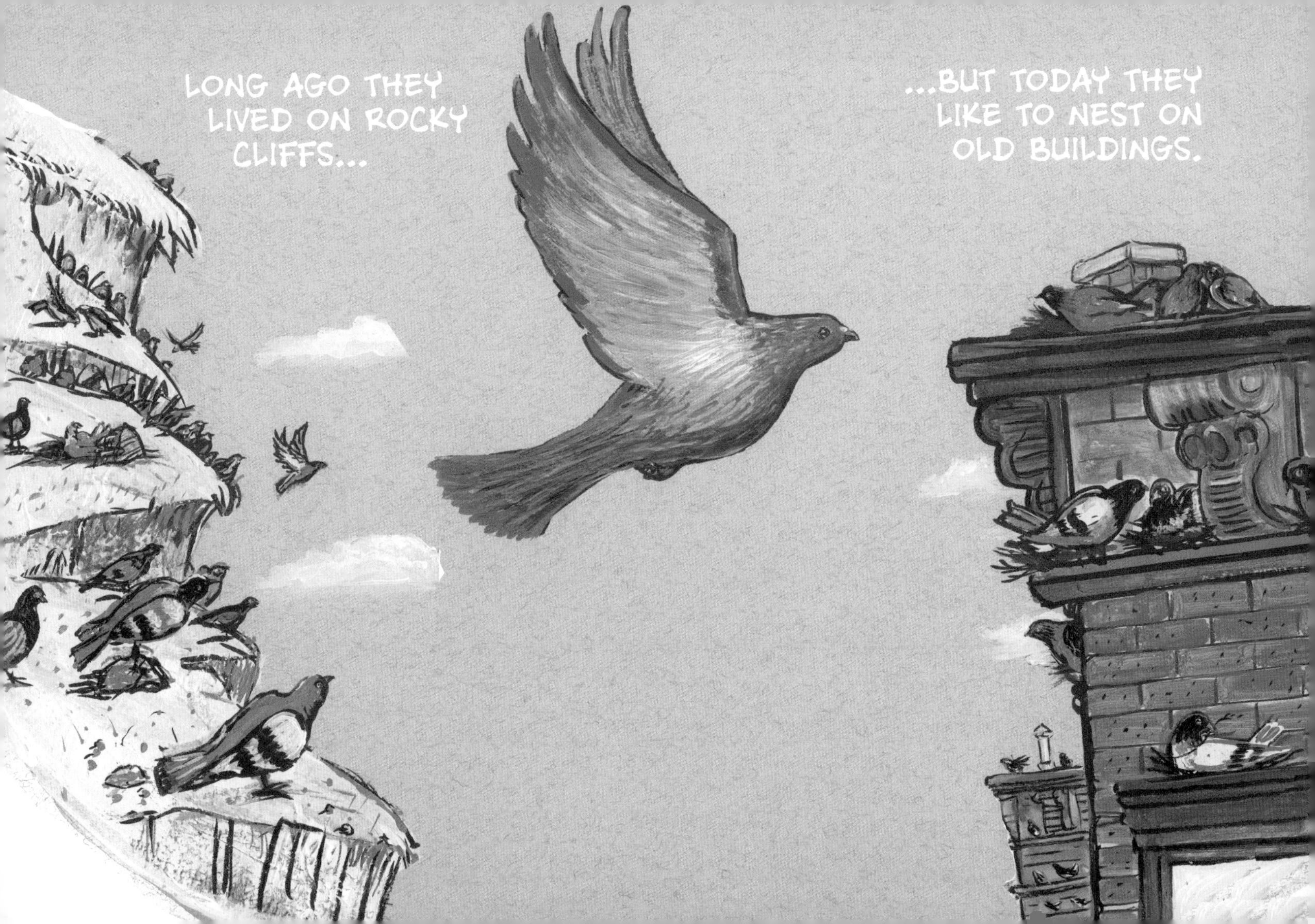
LONG AGO THEY LIVED ON ROCKY CLIFFS...
...BUT TODAY THEY LIKE TO NEST ON OLD BUILDINGS.

WHEN TWO PIGEONS
MAKE A FAMILY,
THAT'S CALLED
MATING.

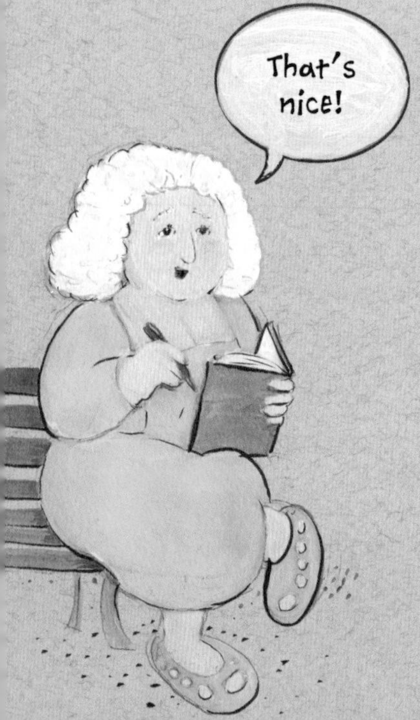
That's nice!

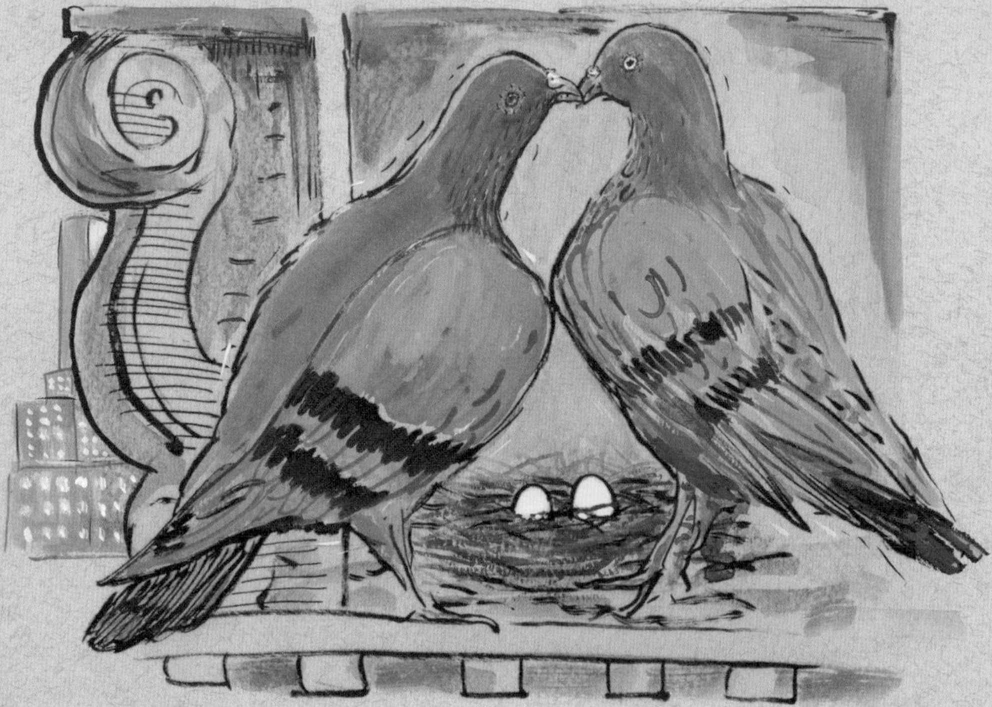

PIGEONS MATE FOR LIFE.

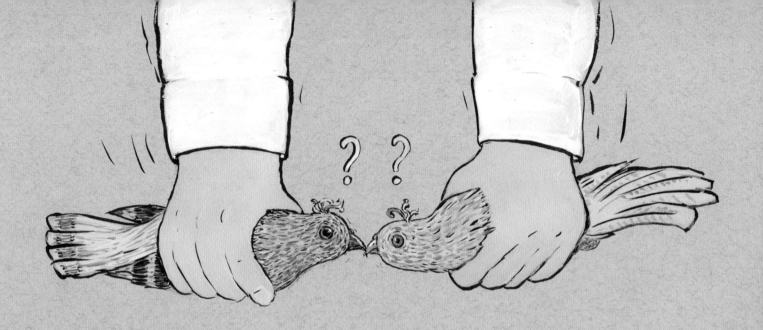

IF A HUMAN PICKS THE TWO PIGEONS TO MATE, THAT IS CALLED **BREEDING**.

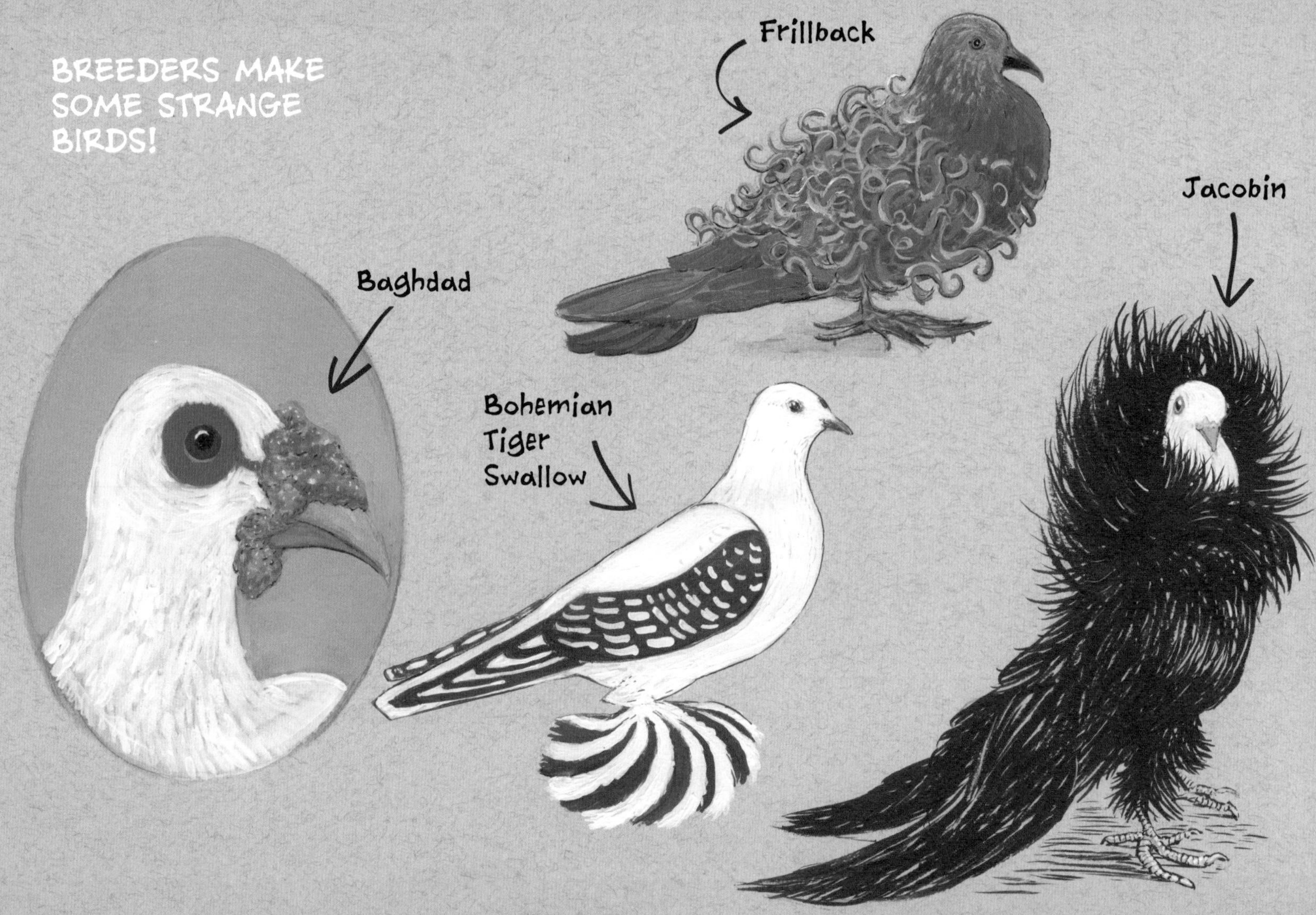
BREEDERS MAKE SOME STRANGE BIRDS!
Frillback
Jacobin
Baghdad
Bohemian Tiger Swallow

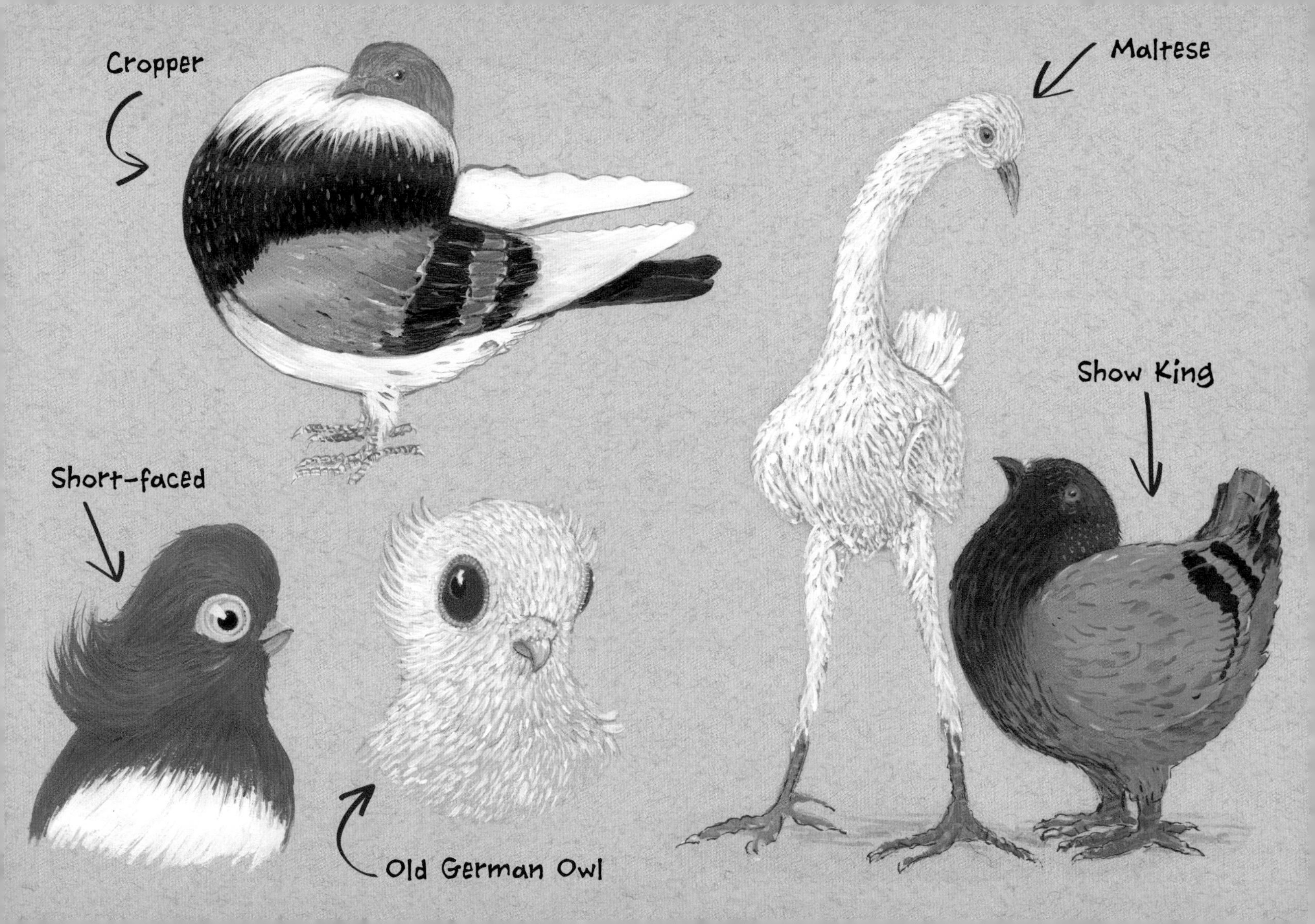
Cropper
Maltese
Show King
Short-faced
Old German Owl

THE FANTAIL
IS A
PRETTY
PIGEON.

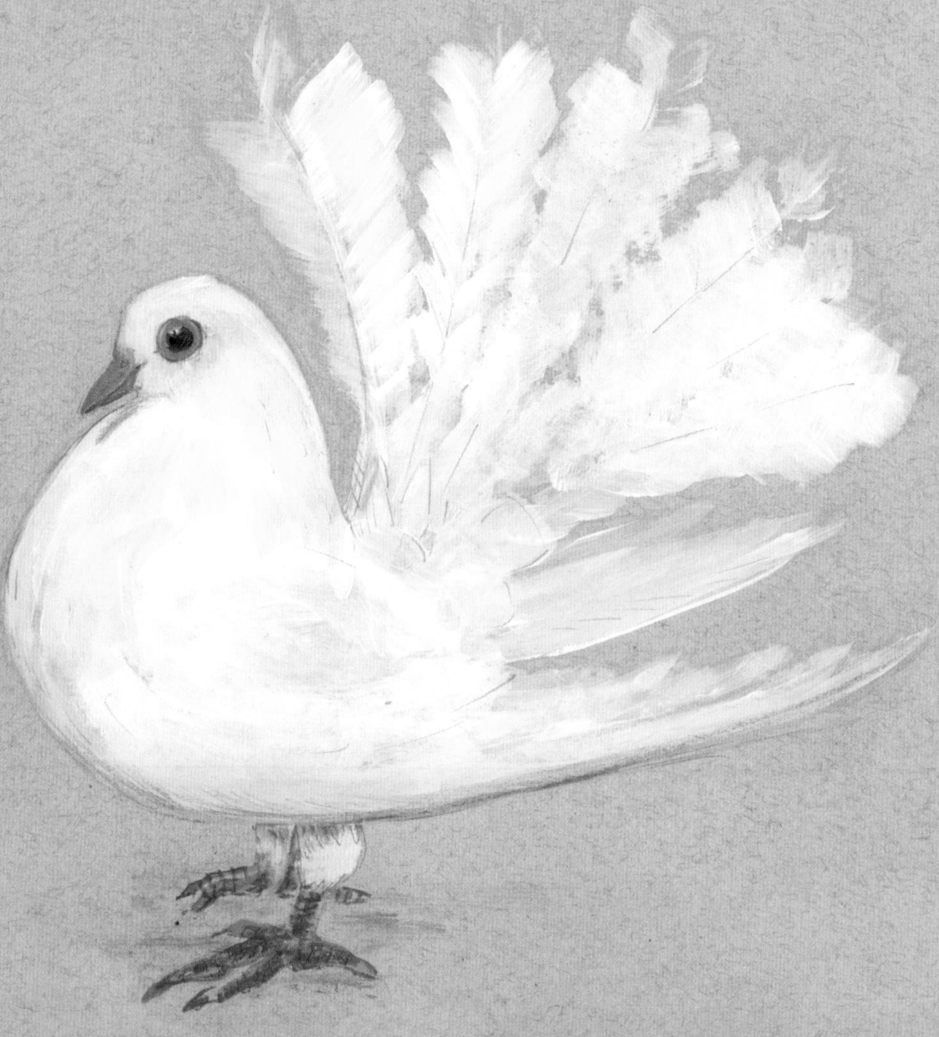

FANCIES
ARE PIGEONS
THAT LOOK
FANCY!

THE VICTORIA CROWNED
IS THE **BIGGEST**
LIVING PIGEON.

IT IS NAMED FOR
QUEEN VICTORIA
OF ENGLAND.

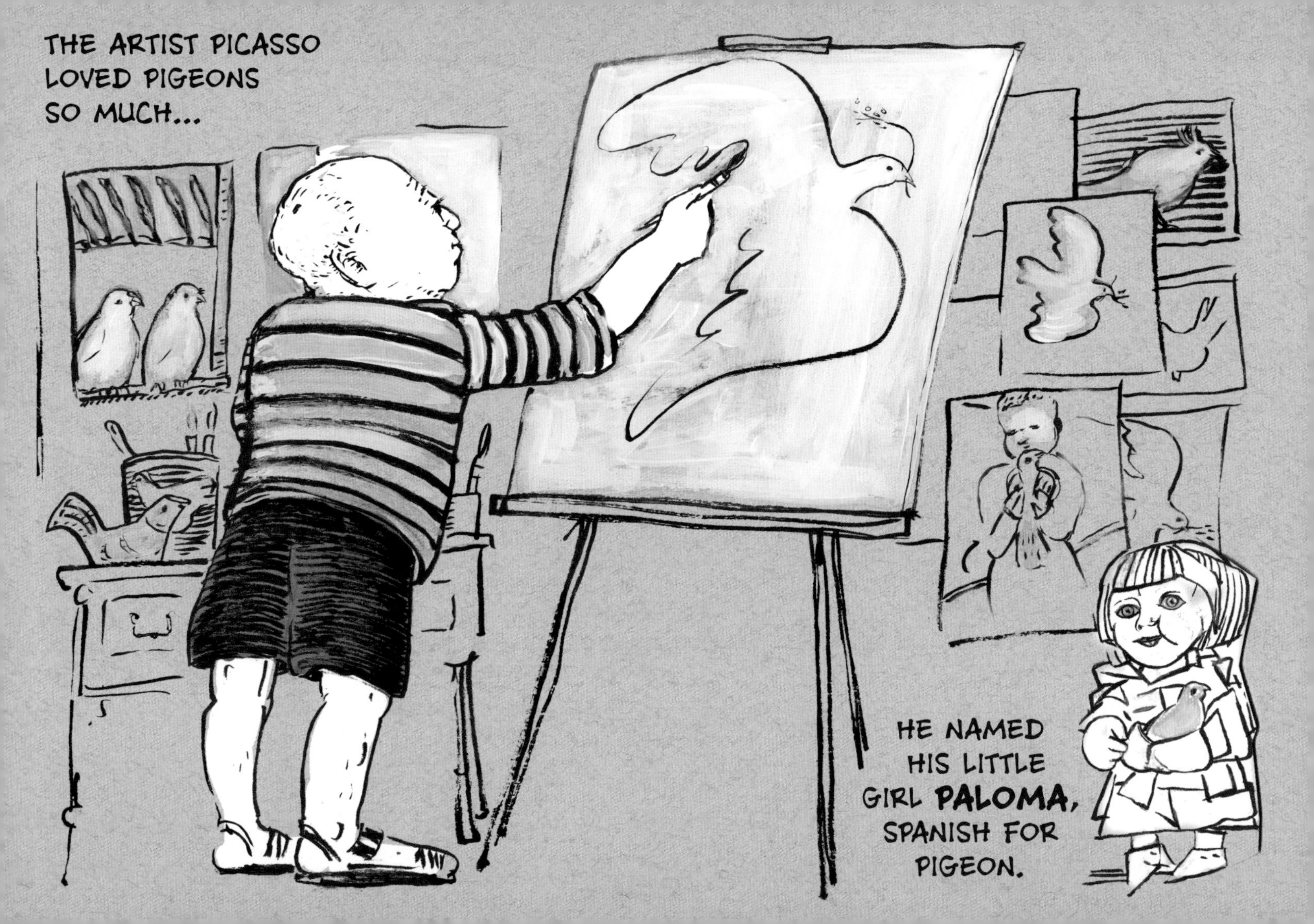
THE ARTIST PICASSO LOVED PIGEONS SO MUCH...
HE NAMED HIS LITTLE GIRL **PALOMA**, SPANISH FOR PIGEON.

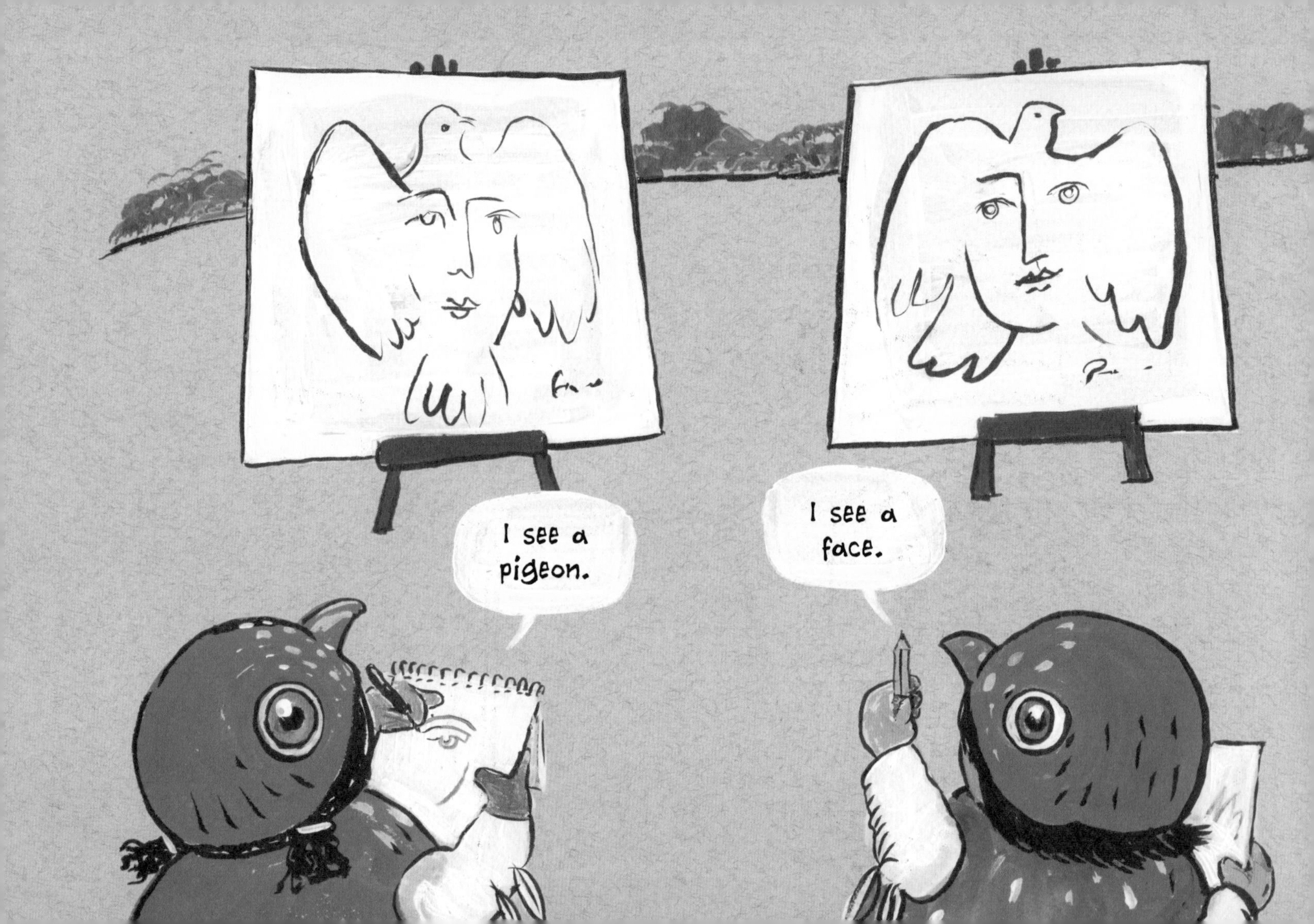
I see a pigeon.
I see a face.

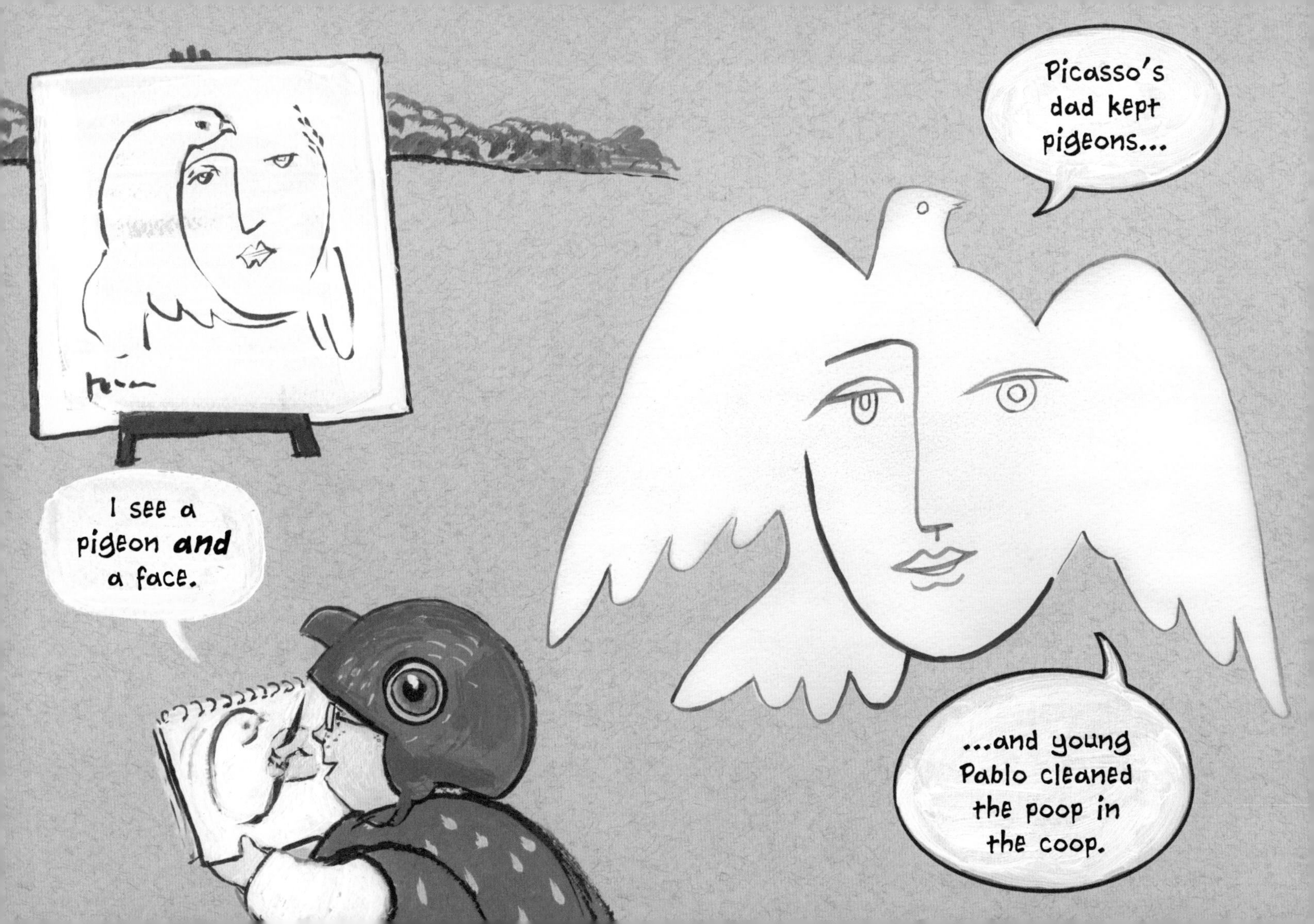
I see a pigeon **and** a face.
Picasso's dad kept pigeons...
...and young Pablo cleaned the poop in the coop.

SOME PIGEONS
CAN BE **VERY** BIG.
THE **DODO** WAS
THREE FEET TALL.

Dodo
-pigeon family-
Last Seen
-1662-

Much too
big to fly!

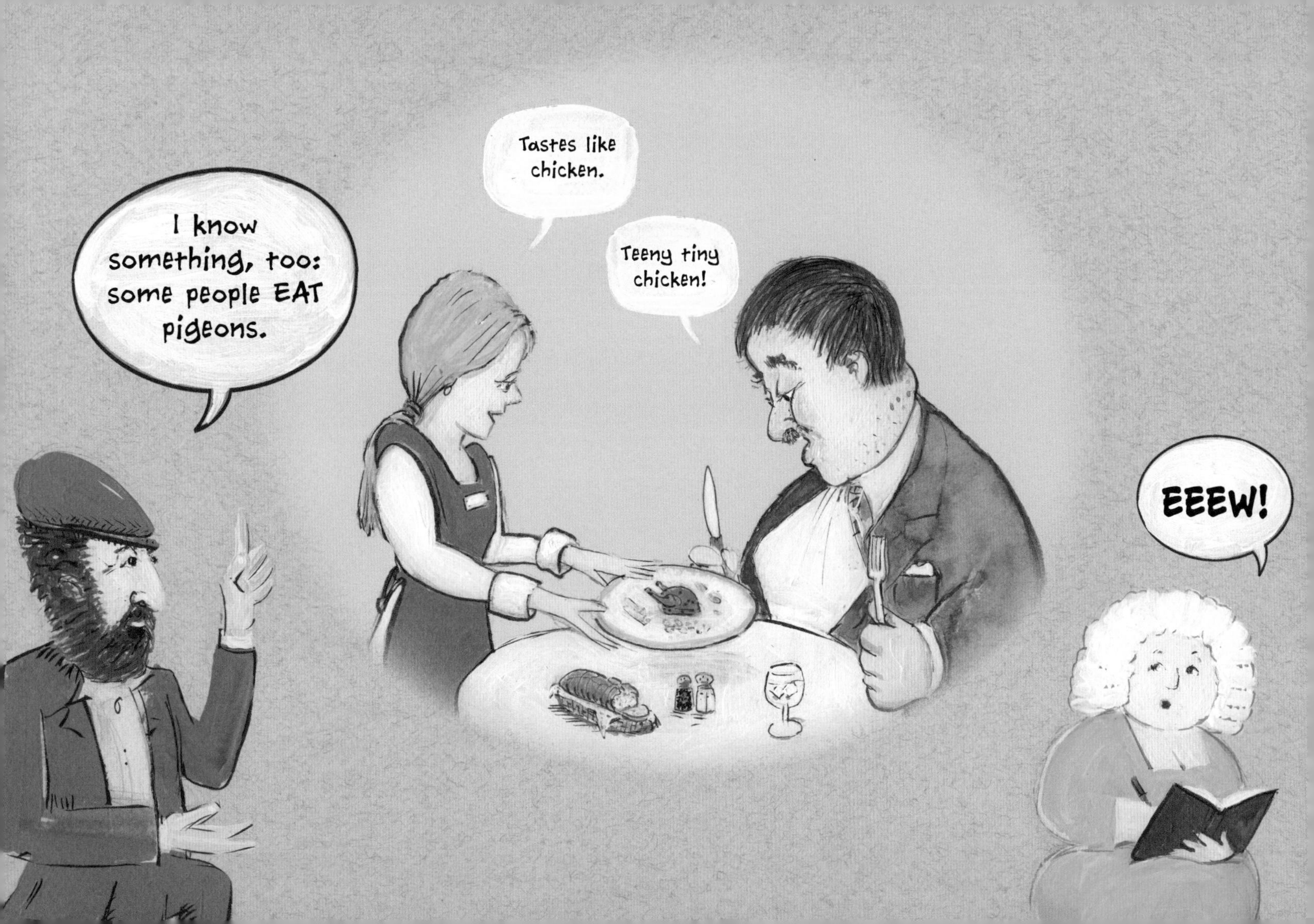
I know something, too: some people EAT pigeons.
Tastes like chicken.
Teeny tiny chicken!
EEEW!

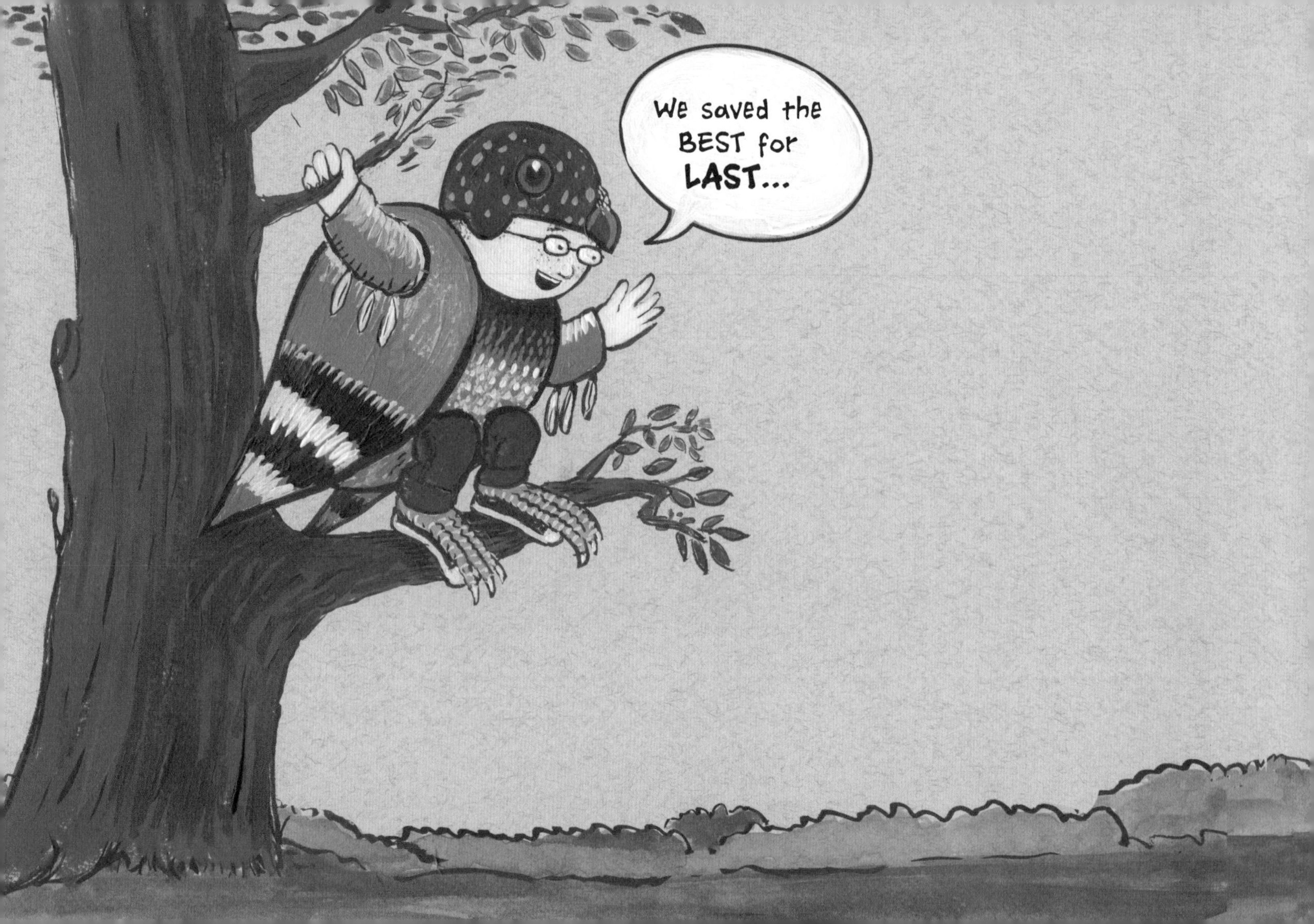
We saved the BEST for LAST...

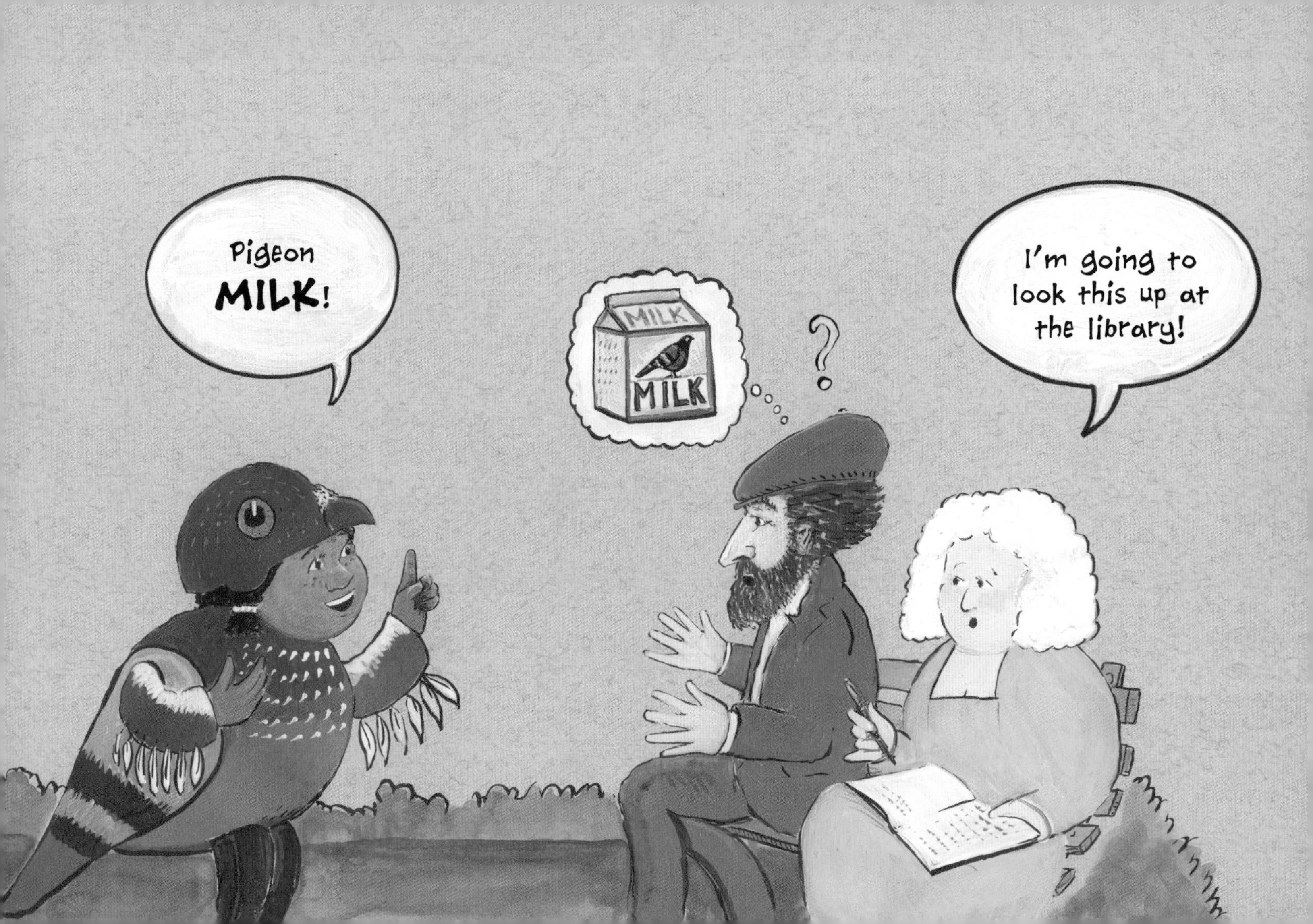
Pigeon MILK!
MILK
MILK
?
I'm going to look this up at the library!

PIGEON MILK DOES **NOT** COME FROM A MOTHER'S BREAST.

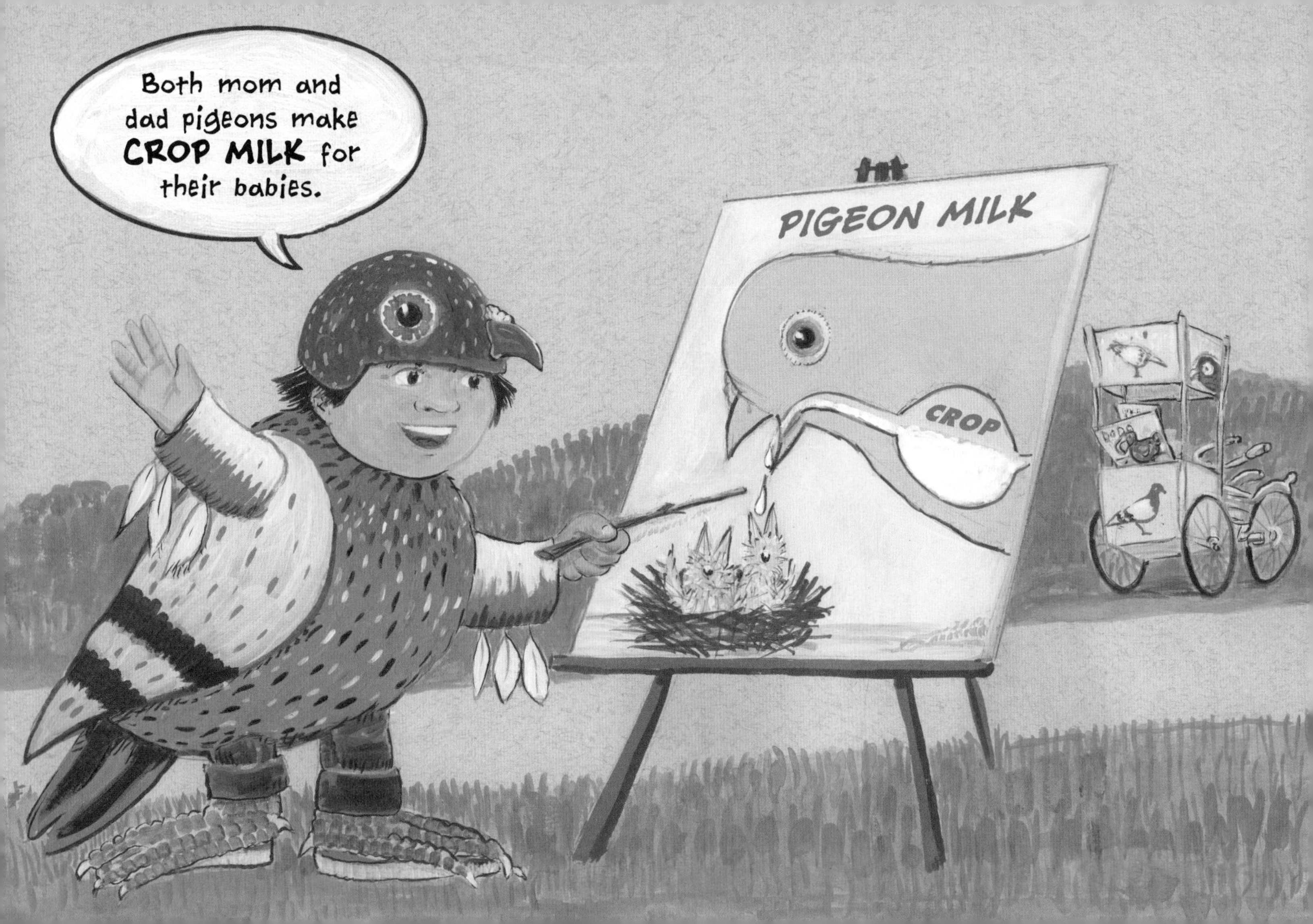
Both mom and dad pigeons make **CROP MILK** for their babies.
PIGEON MILK
CROP

A FEW OTHER BIRDS MAKE CROP MILK FOR THEIR CHICKS.

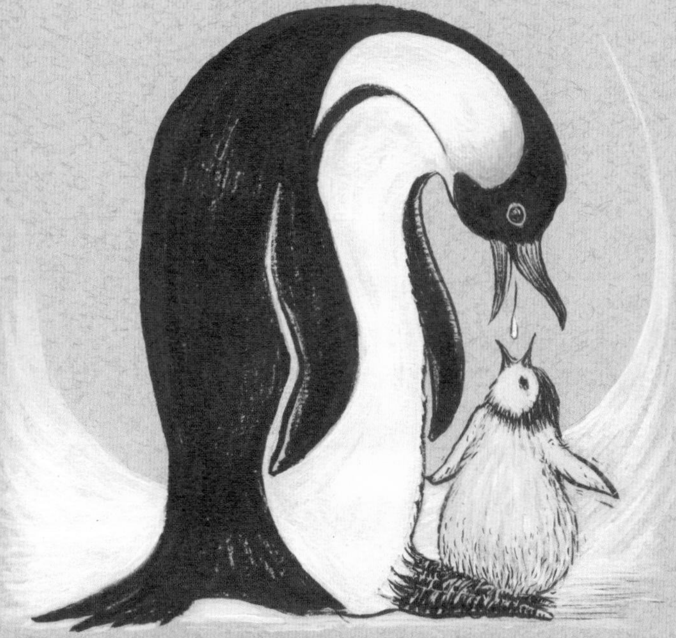

EMPEROR PENGUINS

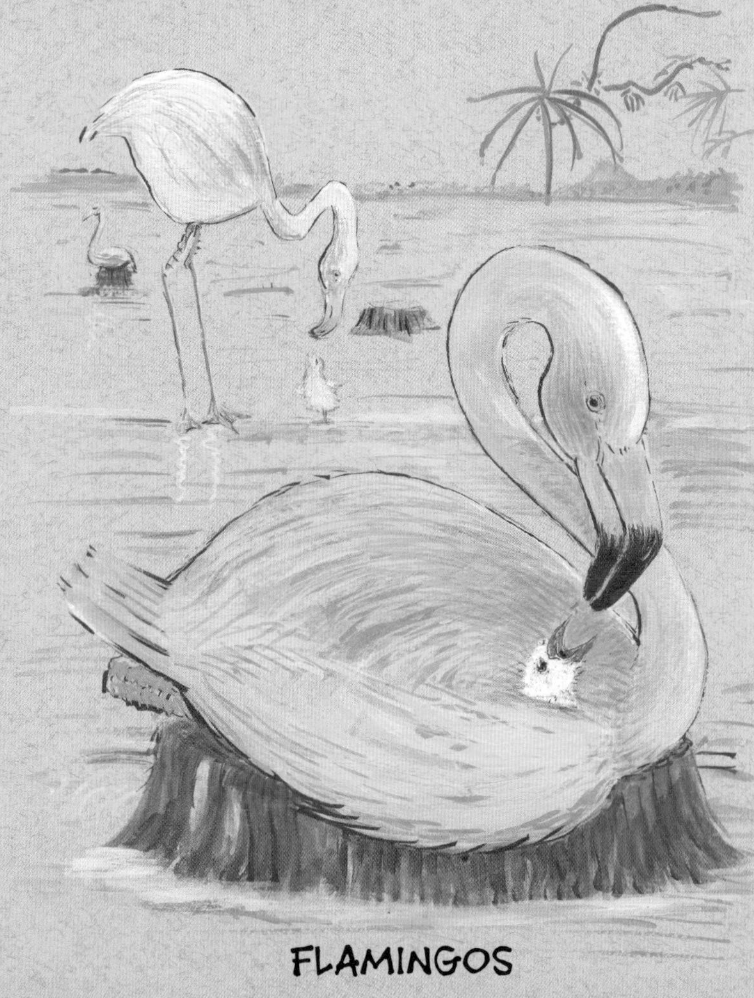

FLAMINGOS

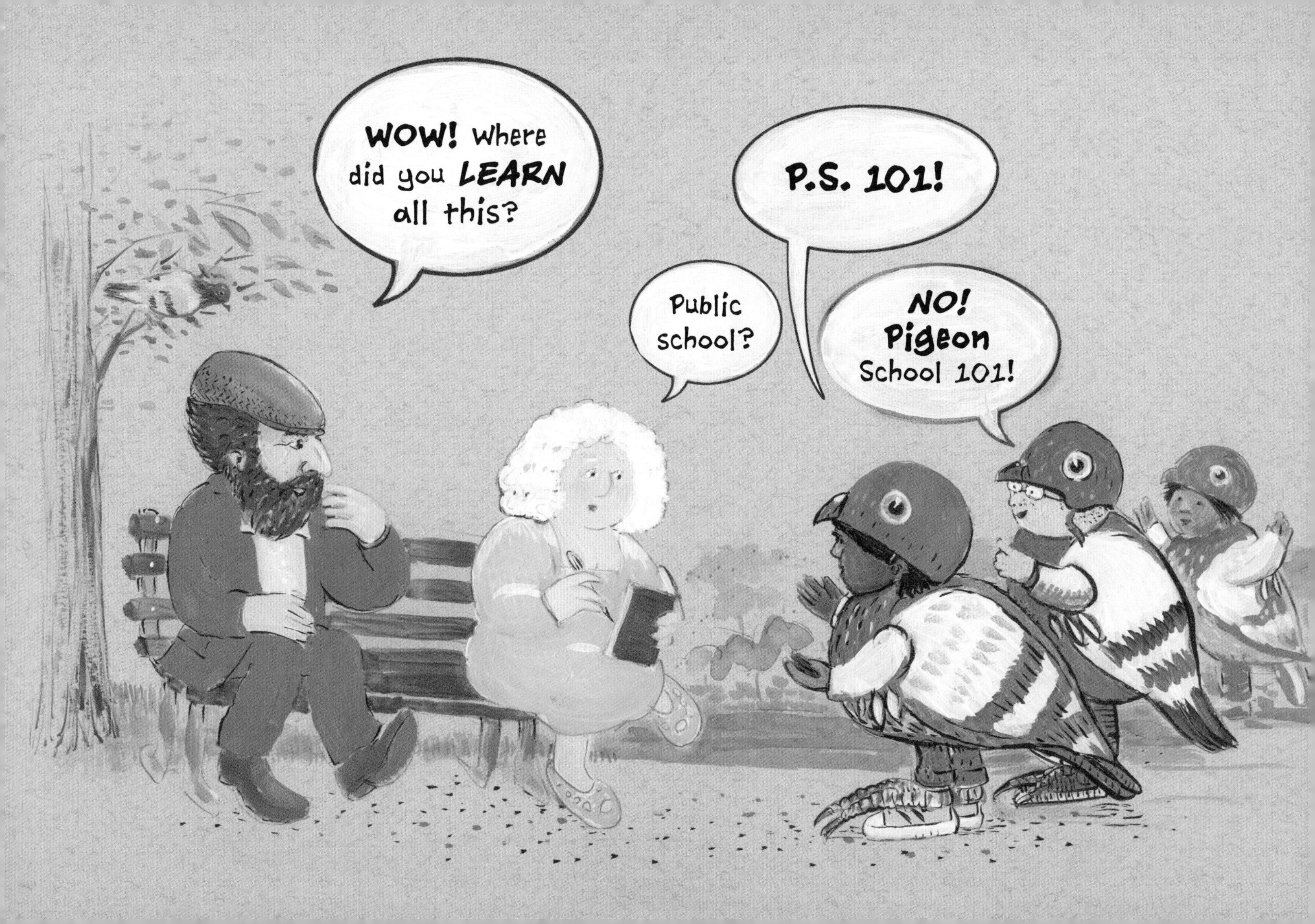
WOW! Where did you LEARN all this?
Public school?
P.S. 101!
NO! Pigeon School 101!

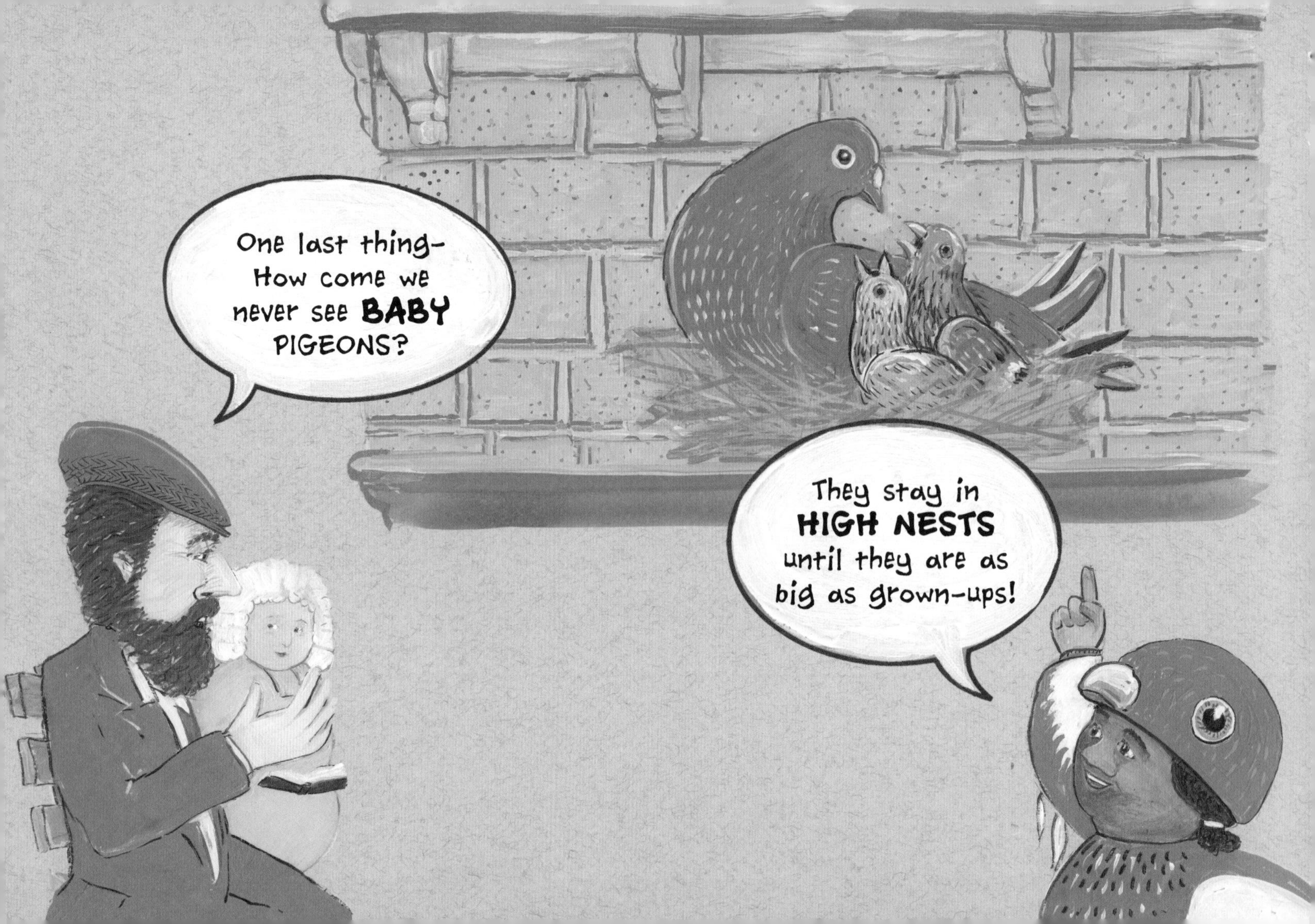
One last thing- How come we never see **BABY** PIGEONS?
They stay in **HIGH NESTS** until they are as big as grown-ups!

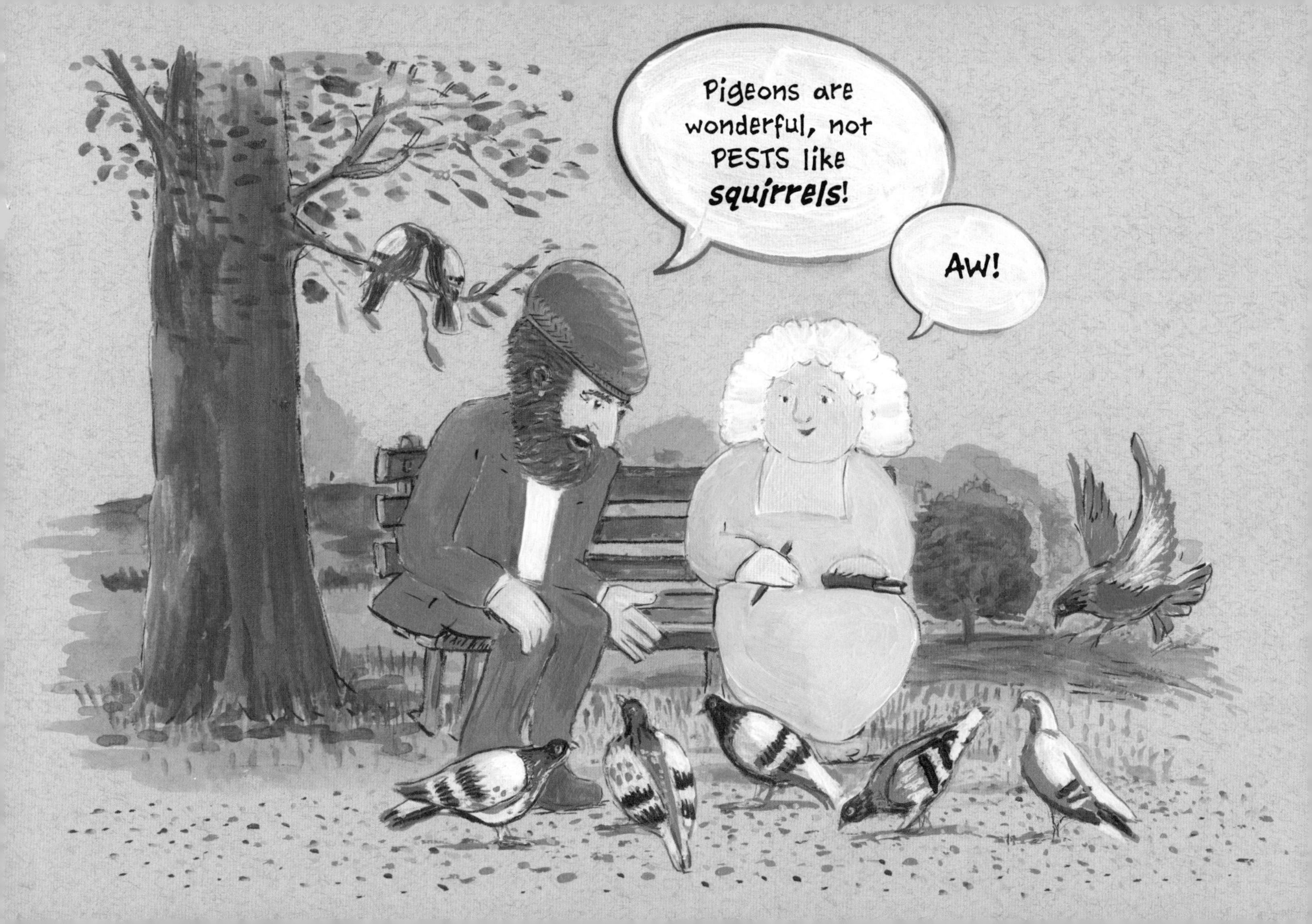
Pigeons are wonderful, not PESTS like squirrels!
AW!

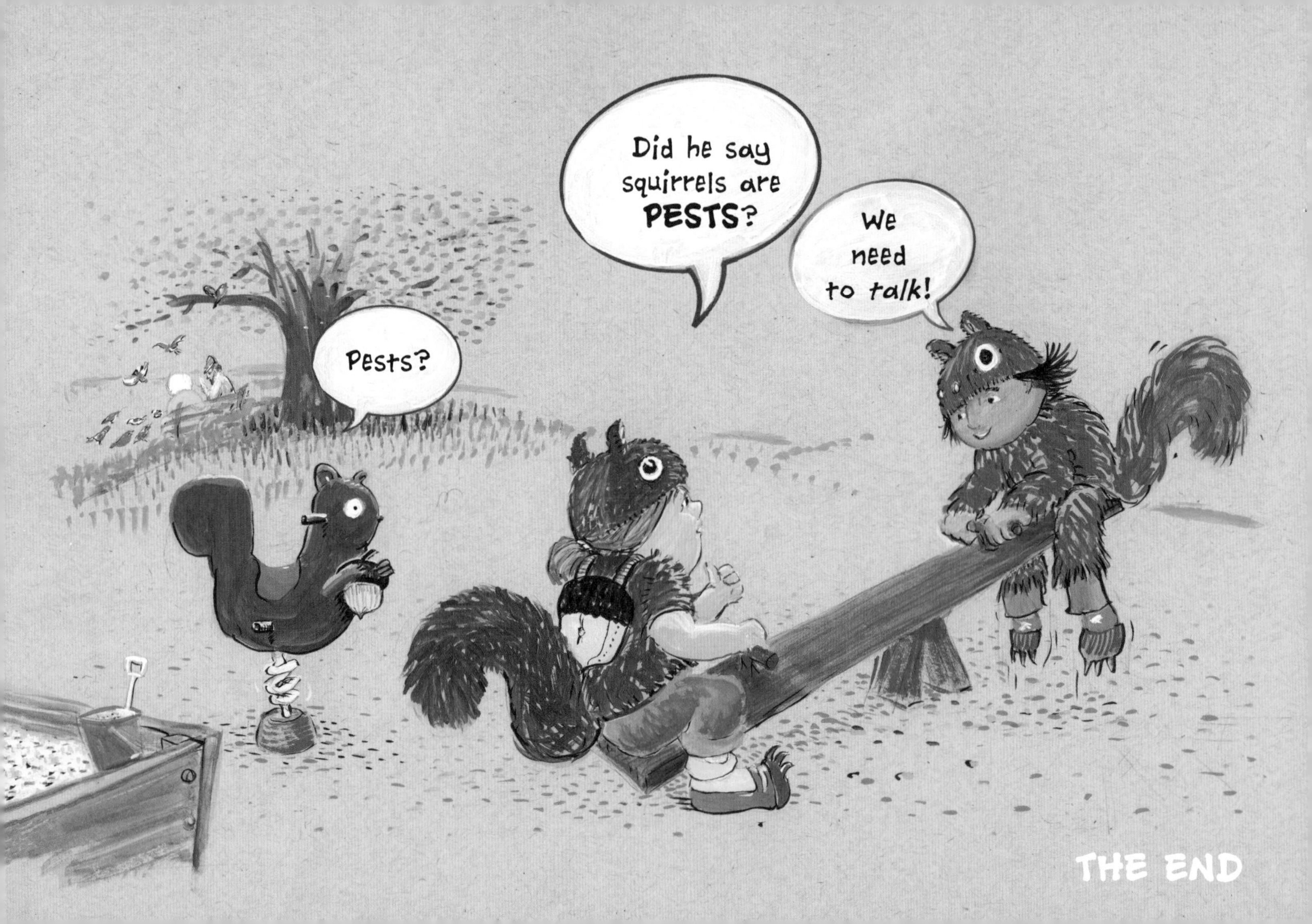
Pests?
Did he say squirrels are PESTS?
We need to talk!
THE END

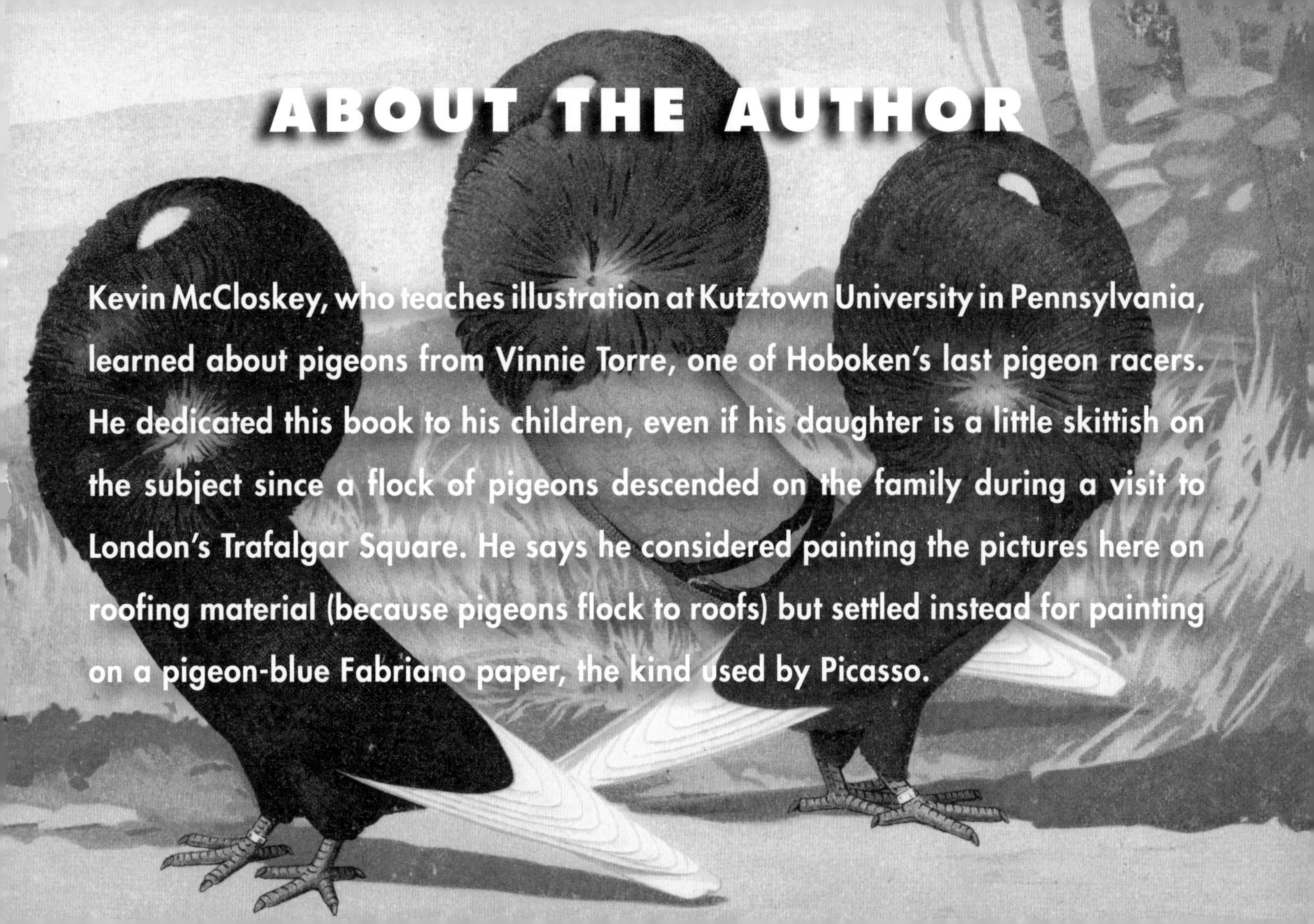

ABOUT THE AUTHOR

Kevin McCloskey, who teaches illustration at Kutztown University in Pennsylvania, learned about pigeons from Vinnie Torre, one of Hoboken's last pigeon racers. He dedicated this book to his children, even if his daughter is a little skittish on the subject since a flock of pigeons descended on the family during a visit to London's Trafalgar Square. He says he considered painting the pictures here on roofing material (because pigeons flock to roofs) but settled instead for painting on a pigeon-blue Fabriano paper, the kind used by Picasso.

HOW TO READ COMICS WITH KIDS

Kids love comics! They are naturally drawn to the details in the pictures, which make them want to read the words. Comics beg for repeated readings and let both emerging and reluctant readers enjoy complex stories with a rich vocabulary. But since comics have their own grammar, here are a few tips for reading them with kids:

GUIDE YOUNG READERS: Use your finger to show your place in the text, but keep it at the bottom of the speaking character so it doesn't hide the very important facial expressions.

HAM IT UP! Think of the comic book story as a play and don't hesitate to read with expression and intonation. Assign parts or get kids to supply the sound effects, a great way to reinforce phonics skills.

LET THEM GUESS. Comics provide lots of context for the words, so emerging readers can make informed guesses. Like jigsaw puzzles, comics ask readers to make connections, so check a young audience's understanding by asking "What's this character thinking?" (but don't be surprised if a kid finds some of the comics' subtle details faster than you).

TALK ABOUT THE PICTURES. Point out how the artist paces the story with pauses (silent panels) or speeded-up action (a burst of short panels). Discuss how the size and shape of the panels carry meaning.

ABOVE ALL, ENJOY! There is of course never one right way to read, so go for the shared pleasure. Once children make the story happen in their imagination, they have discovered the thrill of reading, and you won't be able to stop them. At that point, just go get them more books, and more comics.

www.TOON-BOOKS.com

SEE OUR FREE ONLINE CARTOON MAKERS, LESSON PLANS, AND MUCH MORE